the lonely heart of MAYBELLE LANE

the lonely heart of MAYBELLE LANE

Kate O'Shaughnessy

ALFRED A. KNOPF

New York

THIS IS A BORZOI BOOK PUBLISHED BY ALFRED A. KNOPF

Visit us on the Web! rhcbooks.com

Educators and librarians, for a variety of teaching tools, visit us at RHTeachersLibrarians.com

Library of Congress Cataloging-in-Publication Data is available upon request.

ISBN 978-1-9848-9383-3 (trade) — ISBN 978-1-9848-9384-0 (lib. bdg.) — ISBN 978-1-9848-9385-7 (ebook)

The text of this book is set in 12.75-point Dante.
Interior design by Trish Parcell

Printed in the United States of America
March 2020
10 9 8 7 6 5 4 3 2 1

First Edition

This book is dedicated to anyone who's ever felt lonely.
You're not nearly as alone as you think.

CHAPTER 1

Most people don't think fate has a sound.

But it does. Everything has a sound if you listen carefully enough.

For example: Loneliness sounds like the *drip-drop* of a leaky faucet, or the *clomp* of footsteps in an empty parking lot. Dread is the *vrr-vrr-vrr* of a car engine that won't start. Love is the sound of Momma strumming her guitar and singing softly beneath her breath. And happiness? At the time, I didn't know what the sound of happiness was. I hadn't found it yet.

As for fate, I imagine no two individual fates sound exactly the same. Yours might be the rip of an envelope or the ringing of a phone in the middle of the night. Mine arrived sounding like the deep, night-sky purr of a voice on the radio. Though, of course, I didn't know it was my fate at the time.

Fate was the last thing on my mind that afternoon. It was the second week of summer vacation, and Momma and I were in the car on our way to the Shop 'n Save. I had a plastic bag full of coupons sticking to my bare legs, and the plastic beads on my necklace were *knicker-knack*ing in the hot, soupy breeze coming in through my window.

I usually loved trips to the Shop 'n Save. We went twice a month, and Momma let me pick out one special snack just for me, no matter how unhealthy it was. I would spend the whole car ride thinking about what I wanted. Sometimes I chose a king-size bag of Skittles (I always saved the orange ones for Momma), and other times, I got a box of Ritz Crackers and a can of Easy Cheese.

But on that afternoon, the only thing I could think about was the torn top of Momma's special letter, sticking out of one of the cup holders. I could tell it was the only thing she could think about, too, because she kept running her fingers over its ragged edge, like she wanted to reassure herself it was real.

Maybe she could tell my thoughts were in a stormy swirl, because she reached out and squeezed my hand. "May, I won't do it. Not if you don't want me to. Three weeks is a long time for me to be gone—"

"No," I said. "You have to do it. I'll be fine. I swear."

The letter was from the director of entertainment for Royale Cruises, and it was about a job as a musician on their fanciest ship, *Heart of the Sea*. Momma had auditioned for it on a whim, after someone who heard her playing at the Pit Stop Bar & Bar-B-Que had handed her a business card.

Getting this job was her dream. It could be her big break, she told me, plus they were paying almost as much for three weeks' work as Momma usually made in three months. She had no formal training, so she figured she was the unlikeliest person on the planet to get the position.

But she was wrong. Because here was the letter offering her a contract. She'd be going on a bunch of short cruises, shuttling back and forth between Miami and the Bahamas. The letter said she had to be in Miami for crew training in a few weeks.

Three whole weeks. I'd never been without her for much more than a night. Two, at most.

I tried to ignore the tightness in my chest, the painful and heavy thumping of my heart. I couldn't fall apart, not when she was so happy. So I forced myself to smile. "I'm excited for you, Momma. I'll be fine."

"Maybe I could ask your gram to come stay?"

Now *that* made my smile into something real. I hadn't seen Gram in a long time. Too long. "Really? You think she would?"

"I hope so." She smiled back at me. "Thank you for

being so understanding. Think what we can do with all that money. And, who knows, maybe this will open more doors. Maybe I can quit answering phones at the auto shop. Maybe they'll want me to come back and play on some other cruises, too."

The hope in her voice sounded bright and full, like birdsong.

"Maybe," I agreed, but all I could think was how that meant even more weeks and months without Momma might loom in my future. I hoped she was only getting caught up in the moment. I stared out the window and focused on my breathing, a long inhale and a long exhale.

Momma drummed her fingers against the steering wheel and hummed a happy tune to herself. After a minute of this, she said, "Hey, pretty, will you put some music on? If you don't, I'm going to burst out singing myself."

I must not have responded fast enough, because she tilted her head back and sang out, *"She came to me on a cold, dark night. . . ."*

"Not that song," I said quickly. "Please."

That was the first line to the bedtime song she sang to me every night when I was little. She wrote it for me when I was born.

"Oh, won't you sing it with me, just once? I haven't heard that gorgeous voice of yours in so long. Too long."

I shook my head. The thought of singing in front of someone else ever again—even Momma—made me feel sick to my stomach. "No. Not right now."

"Okay," she said, drawing the word out with a sigh. "Fine. If you won't sing, then be a love and flip on the radio."

I turned to stare at her. "You want me to turn on the radio? The *radio*?"

She shrugged as she slowed down at a light and turned on the blinker. "I was cleaning out the car this morning, and I forgot to put the Bible back in."

Momma rarely forgot her Bible, which was her name for the binder of CDs she kept stashed in the back seat. Our car was old, which meant we had no way of connecting Momma's phone to its speakers. So we'd spent weekends together scouring thrift shops, looking for her favorites. The Bible had been built up over years. She loved all sorts of music—country, folk, rock, hip-hop, classical, and even that metal stuff, which reminded me of chain saws and the unpleasant screech of chalk on a blackboard. But out of all the music she listened to, she loved the blues the most. She liked the old-fashioned twangy blues of Guitar Slim and Snooks Eaglin and also the rich, sometimes growly crooning of John Lee Hooker, Johnny Adams, and Albert Collins. Memphis Minnie, B. B. King, Bessie Smith . . . the list went on and on.

But never the radio. For whatever reason, she'd always had a "thing" against the radio, ever since I was little.

"Well, all right." I reached forward to turn it on. "If you say so."

Static came out first. On the next station, some angry preacher was hollering about the Lord this and the devil that and something about hellfire, so I pressed the button again. Next was a pop song with a thumping beat. I looked at Momma, but she made a face, so I went to the next station.

And that's when I heard it. The sound of my fate coming up to meet me.

I could hardly blink or breathe or think. It wasn't music. It was a voice. Not even singing . . . just talking.

Even though the car's speakers were old and tinny, the sound of the man's voice that filled the car was like . . . well, it was like magic. It was the purr of a house cat and the roar of a lion. It was the thrum of the lowest piano key, like velvet and gravel and the deepest, darkest part of the night sky, all at once.

Then that voice *laughed*. It made me feel like laughing myself, like the whole car had been lit up with rays of sunshine.

And that's when I realized how familiar it sounded.

I *knew* that laugh. I knew that laugh deep in my bones.

Momma must have realized it, too, because she made

a strange, strangled noise in the back of her throat and flicked off the radio.

But it was too late.

"Momma," I breathed. I turned to look at her, but she wouldn't meet my eyes. "That was my daddy's voice, wasn't it?"

CHAPTER 2

It was like a ghost come back to life.

I'd asked so many questions about him but had always been met by Momma's stony silence.

What did my daddy do for work? I would ask. *What was his name? Was he handsome? Do I have aunts and uncles, and maybe even cousins my age?* Momma was an only child, so I didn't have any of that on her side. *Could I meet them, Momma?* I'd asked. *Could I?*

But my questions seemed to make something deep down inside Momma hurt. She'd shake her head and say, *I don't want to talk about this. We're better off without all of that.*

I didn't even know his name. The only thing I had of his was a voicemail he left for Momma before I was born. It was on an old cell phone of hers, which Momma kept stowed away in the junk drawer with all the other old-fashioned things she didn't use anymore, like paper maps and a couple of DVDs.

Hey, Gem, he said. *I have this joke to tell you. Oh, man, is it a good one. Call me back when you can.* And then, before he hung up, he laughed, like he was remembering the joke himself. He had a booming laugh that burst out of the phone and filled the air with warmth, the way it feels when you close your eyes and lift your face to the sun.

He *had* to be kind, I told myself. No one had a laugh that warm who wasn't also kind. And he was probably funny. The day after I found that voicemail, I took out a joke book from the library at school. I couldn't help but wonder if the ones that made me laugh would make my daddy laugh, too.

I played it over and over again so many times that I wore out the flip phone's battery. I begged Momma to get it fixed. I didn't tell her it was so I could keep listening to my daddy's voicemail, though I suspected she knew.

"It's so I have a way to call you when you're working," I told her. "Lots of kids in my grade have phones."

After some hemming and hawing, Momma finally agreed and went to fix up the battery and get the phone connected to her account. But when she brought it back, the voicemail was gone.

I kept turning the phone on and off, praying the message would reappear, but it never did.

"I'm so sorry, May," she said. "They must have cleared the data without me realizing it."

Even though she *sounded* sorry, part of me suspected she had them delete it on purpose. But I never asked her about it. I couldn't bear to.

After I lost the one thing connecting me to him, I stopped asking so many questions. I let go of the daydreams. I imagined that maybe my daddy was an astronaut in outer space, far, far away. And the less I asked about him, the happier Momma got.

But now here he was. Talking and laughing on the radio.

"That was him, wasn't it?" I asked again.

By then she had pulled our car to the shoulder. Our hazard lights were flashing and *click-click-click*ing, steady as a heartbeat. "Maybelle . . ."

She didn't even have to answer. Her voice gave her away.

She started rubbing her face, so when she spoke again, her voice was muffled. "The *one* day I turn the radio on."

A million questions bubbled up right away.

Why was he on the radio? Was he one of those radio DJs? Is that why Momma hated the radio so much?

If he was a DJ, why hadn't I heard his voice before, in the gas station or the grocery store?

Was he local? Or was he on a national program?

I reached forward to turn the radio on again, but Momma put her hand in front of it. "May, don't. Just don't. I never wanted him in our lives, which is why I never told him about you in the first place."

I already knew she had never told my daddy about me being born, and there was nothing I could do about that. But now that I knew he was a real live person and not an idea in my head, everything felt different. "Yeah, well, maybe you should."

She shook her head. "No. And I'm not going to change my mind about that."

"But *why?*" I asked. "I don't understand."

"Because he broke my heart, and I don't want him to get the chance to break yours. Which is why I want you to promise me you won't go looking for any more information about your daddy. Nothing good will come of it." She reached out and squeezed my hand, a desperate look on her face. "Please, May. Promise me. He'll only break your heart."

The worry and pain in her voice almost knocked me over. So I nodded.

CHAPTER 3

But I didn't *promise*. Not out loud.

I couldn't. It wouldn't matter if I made a million promises. Now that he was within reach, I'd never be able to forget about my daddy or his golden voice, no matter how hard I tried.

Momma worked two jobs, so for most of my days and nights that summer, I was home alone and free to roam Pelican Park, the trailer court where we lived, as much as I pleased. A few days after I heard my daddy's voice, I walked to the pawnshop a mile down the road and used up what little savings I had to buy myself a radio.

On the way there, the Louisiana summer air pressed against my skin like a dog's hot breath. I was sweaty within minutes, but the heat bothered me less than all the thoughts whirling in my head. My whole life, I'd never really blamed Momma for the fact that I'd never met my daddy. I kept them in completely different buckets—daydreams about my daddy in one, and real life with Momma in another. We rarely fought or got mad at each other about anything. To me, her word was final.

But now that I'd heard him talking and laughing in real time, on a live radio program, the two buckets had morphed into one.

The reason I didn't know my daddy was *because of* Momma. *She'd* kept us apart.

From the one or two questions she had answered, she'd made it sound like he wasn't a bad person. Only that it hadn't ended well between them. So why was she doing this? Why wasn't she giving me a chance to know him—and him a chance to know *me*?

How could she? How *dare* she?

But at the same time, I didn't want her to know I felt like this. I didn't want to fight at all, because I didn't want to push her away. Not even an inch. If anything, I almost wanted to squeeze her closer—even with a hot coal of anger in my chest. Because most of the time, especially since we'd moved to Davenport, she was all I had.

So while I hated going behind Momma's back like this, it wasn't enough to stop me. If anything, it made us even. Because she'd done wrong, too.

"Oh, you're lucky," the salesclerk said, once I told him what I was looking for. He reached below the case and unlocked it. He had skin like old leather, and as he leaned over the counter to hand me something, I got a fierce whiff of stale cigarette smoke. "This here's a vintage AM/FM Gran Prix pocket radio. Very rare, since it still works. We don't get these old things in much anymore."

I took the pocket radio from the counter and weighed it in my hand. It was a perfect fit. Even its name sent tingles down my spine. Gran Prix.

"How much?" I asked.

"Fifteen."

I only had eleven dollars. I tried my best to keep the wobble from my voice as I told him so.

The clerk looked at me for a long time before he nodded. "Well, all right. That's a steal for this product, but I can see in your eyes that the two of you are meant to be."

I grinned the entire walk home, clutching the radio to my chest like it might fly away if I wasn't careful. With every step I took, a whole new world opened up in front of me. It was just after noon, which was around the time I'd heard my daddy a couple days before, so as soon as I got home, I sat on the couch and flipped through the stations until I found WKBC 101.3. Ever since I'd heard him in the car, I'd repeated the station's name in my head a hundred times to make sure I'd never forget it.

And he was on!

Suddenly the room felt like it was lit up with shooting stars. He was talking to a listener named Shawna.

It hadn't been a dream. I really had heard him in the car. He was real.

"He doesn't listen to me anymore," Shawna was saying. "At supper it's like I'm talking to a crash-test dummy instead of a real live person. I feel invisible half the time."

"Sometimes it feels like the world is full of people who don't understand us, who don't listen to us, don't you think?" he rumbled in his velvet voice. "But that's what I'm here for. To listen. So, Shawna, tell me. How was your day?"

Shawna went on and on. And my daddy listened. *Really* listened. He never hustled her off the air. He laughed in all the right places. By the end of their conversation, she had a smile in her voice, and I swear I could almost feel her blushing through the radio.

It only made me want more. But I didn't want to learn about Shawna. I wanted to learn about *him*.

So I leaned back and was settling in for the rest of his show when I heard the sound of keys scrabbling in the lock. Usually this was a good sound. The best sound, because it meant Momma was home.

But not today. Today she was home early from her morning shift at the auto shop. Of all days!

Our front door was swollen from the muggy summer heat, so it took her a couple good pushes to swing it open. This gave me just enough time to flick the radio off and hide it beneath the couch cushions.

"Hey! Hi!" I said. "What are you doing home?"

"I asked Jay if I could get off early," Momma said. "I wanted to surprise you. I thought we could go to the Burger Shack for lunch. To celebrate the new job."

"Wow," I said, sliding off the couch. I couldn't help but glance at the cushions. They were already lumpy, but was that an extra-big lump where my radio was? As long as Momma didn't sit down, I thought it'd be okay. "Great. Let's go! We can go right now."

Momma laughed as she shook her long brown hair free from its ponytail. "Okay, Miss Eager Beaver. Let me get out of these clothes. I smell like motor oil and gasoline."

I sat gingerly on the couch, right on top of my radio, while Momma changed. I had to come up with a better hiding spot, because I couldn't let her find out about it. I couldn't let my newfound relationship with my daddy end before it even began.

* ✳ ✦ ✳ *

The Burger Shack was where Momma took me whenever she was feeling guilty about something. She took me twice in one week when we first moved to Davenport from Baton Rouge, and then again when she told me she was taking on another job to help cover the bills.

I probably should've hated it there, but I didn't. We didn't go to restaurants very often, and the Burger Shack had cool retro red leather booths and the best vanilla milkshakes I'd ever tasted.

As I dipped one of my salty fries into my milkshake, I glanced at my watch. How long was my daddy's show? An hour? Two? Would he still be on when I got home? Was he that kind to all the listeners that called in?

"Yuck." Momma wrinkled her nose as I popped the milkshake-covered fry into my mouth. "I'll never understand why you like doing that."

"It's delicious. You should try it," I told her, even though I knew she never would. Momma liked all her foods separated. She didn't even like them touching on the plate.

Could that maybe mean that my daddy dipped his fries into his milkshakes, too? I had to get that trait from *someone*, right? And if it wasn't from Momma, maybe it was from him.

The thought filled me up with light and warmth. Because if we had tiny, small things in common like that, maybe we had big important things in common, too.

"What are you thinking about?" Momma asked. "You have the dreamiest look on your face."

My cheeks went hot. "Nothing."

That's when the door to the burger shop banged

open. It didn't gently ding or chime. It was thrown open with enough force to make it thud against the wall. I turned to see who it was. Jeremiah Johnson, the meanest boy at school, whose words came out like needles and knives. I sank lower in the booth and said a silent prayer he wouldn't see me.

But he did.

He grinned and whispered to the other boys he was with—Tommy O'Brien, who was also in our grade, and Tommy's younger brother Jackson. Tommy and Jackson lived in Pelican Park, too, though I wished they didn't.

Jackson nodded at whatever Jeremiah was saying, and then the three of them came slinking over in our direction. I dropped the fry I was holding back onto my burger wrapper. My appetite had completely disappeared.

"Hey, May," Jeremiah said, that same wicked grin still on his face. "How's your summer been?"

"Fine."

He glanced at Momma. "So is this her? Is this your *famous* momma?"

Next to him, Jackson snickered. Tommy stood a few paces back, his eyes on the floor.

"Famous?" Momma asked. She smiled big at Jeremiah, because I hadn't told her about him or how miserable he'd made my life at school. She looked at me, still smiling. "Why am I famous?"

Before any of them could say anything, I cut in. "Because you're a musician. I've told everyone at school how good you are. That's why you're famous."

But, of course, that wasn't the reason at all. The real reason was that Momma and Miss King, the art teacher at my new school, had gone out on a date. Momma had dated both boys and girls my whole life, so it wasn't that part that bothered me—it was that Miss King was a *teacher.*

And I was scared other people would find out.

I could tell Momma liked her a lot, but I begged her not to see Miss King again. And even though I didn't tell her why I wanted her to stop, Momma listened. She canceled a date with Miss King that very night, and she hadn't been on any dates since. I felt terrible about it. What kind of daughter was I, getting in the way of her happiness?

The worst part was, it didn't end up mattering. Jeremiah found out anyway. I was already the new girl who'd started school a couple months late, and the thing between Momma and Miss King was enough for him to decide I would be his perfect new target.

After Jeremiah set his sights on me, it was like I was contagious with measles or mumps or itchy green boils. One girl, Natalie, sat with me in the library sometimes, but only when no one else was around. Other than that, no one at my new school wanted to touch me with a ten-foot pole. It wasn't worth becoming one of Jeremiah's targets themselves.

Momma pressed her hand to her chest. "Oh, May, you did? You're so sweet."

"Yeah," Jeremiah said, his grin widening. "She's the sweetest little button, isn't she?"

Trashy, Jackson mouthed, behind Momma's head.

I stared at the table and willed the tears to evaporate from my eyes. I would not let them see me cry.

"I'm hungry," Tommy announced loudly from behind them. He started pulling on Jeremiah's shirt. "No, actually, I'm starving. And bored. I'm so bored! Are we getting food or what?"

"Okay, fine, but quit tugging on my shirt like that! You're stretching it out." Jeremiah turned back toward Momma. "It was nice to meet you, Miss Lane," he said, taking her hand and kissing it dramatically.

"Yeah, *so* nice to meet you, Miss Lane!" Jackson called out in a singsongy voice.

Tommy didn't say anything.

Momma watched them head over to the counter to put their orders in. "Are those your friends?"

"*No,*" I said, a bit more forcefully than I meant to.

Momma nodded once, her eyes sharp. "Good. Because I don't like those boys one bit."

"Me neither," I told her. "Can we get out of here?"

"Definitely." Momma crumpled her napkin into a ball and threw it on the table. Then she checked her cell phone and sighed. "I'm working a double, so I should get to work anyway."

CHAPTER 4

As the days ticked by until July seventh, the day of Momma's departure, I decided the best way to distract myself was by throwing myself into my daddy's radio show.

I quickly learned he was the DJ of his own regional show, a brand-new one, broadcasting out of Nashville. It ran four days a week, from eleven to one p.m. Every time his show came on, every time I heard his voice booming out of the radio, it was like sinking into a warm bath.

It didn't take long for me to learn all sorts of things about him.

His name was Richard H. Fitzgerald, and he went by Rick, but all of his co-hosts at WKBC 101.3 called him Fitzy and sometimes Ritzy Fitzy.

He once rescued a raccoon kit from his chimney and named him Hank, after his favorite musician, Hank Williams Jr.

He liked to make nachos with Cool Ranch Doritos instead of corn chips.

I was hungry for the details—even the small ones. I listened to every minute of his show every chance I got. I listened to all the songs he played, even the ones I didn't like.

He wasn't perfect. Not by a long stretch. He picked his teeth on air and said he smoked a pack of Marlboro Red cigarettes a day. Even so, the more I got to know him, the more I got to like him. How could someone so funny and kind and smart break my heart? It didn't make any sense.

Since I'd recently had a special lunch with Momma at the Burger Shack, regardless of how disastrous it'd been, it got me thinking: What would a meal with my daddy be like? Would we laugh at stupid jokes? Would we talk about big important things, like world history or outer space?

So one afternoon, I figured I'd give it a try.

Momma was working another double, so I set the table for two—one spot for me, one for my daddy. I put the radio on the empty chair and turned it to his show. If I squinted, with the lights mostly out and the curtains drawn, I could almost imagine him there, even though I didn't know what he looked like.

I'd been itching to look him up on the internet. Back in Baton Rouge, we had a computer *and* WiFi. Momma had brought her laptop to Davenport, but it mostly sat unused in the living room. Internet was one extra bill we couldn't afford to pay. Momma had a smartphone I could have used, but I was too scared she'd see that I'd looked him up. Sometimes when she fell asleep, her phone on the nightstand next to her, I'd sneak over to her side of the bed and open the phone's internet browser, but I lost my nerve every time.

But I didn't need to know his features to imagine him. His voice filled up so much space, it was like he was really there.

"Would you like some fish sticks, Daddy?" I asked. That was the one food Momma said it was okay to make by myself. That and microwaveable cups of mac and cheese.

I lowered my voice. "Yes, thank you. Did you make these? They look so nice and crispy."

"Yes, I did. More ketchup, Daddy?" I asked, once I'd sat down.

"Oh yes, please, May," I said, lowering my voice again. "I like to drown my fish sticks in ketchup just like you do, to get rid of that awful fishy taste."

I felt silly doing it, like I was playing with dolls even though I knew I was too old.

Then I had an idea: I turned the radio down so his voice became nothing but a murmur, and held it to my ear like a telephone. This felt much more normal. I told him about Momma's jobs at the Pit Stop Bar & Bar-B-Que and Jay's Auto Body Repair, and how badly she wished she could quit and play her guitar full-time instead. I told him it wouldn't be long before she hit it big and we could leave Pelican Park.

I told him how our trailer leaned to the right like a slowly sinking ship, and how much I missed Baton Rouge. I even told him about my sound collection, which, other than Momma and my best friend, Rosa, no one knew about. Not even Gram.

Was this what it would be like if he were around? Instead of ringing silence, would the air be filled with his sunshine laugh? Would he bring me into the radio station and show me off to his friends? Would he ask me to sing so often and so kindly that my fear would go away and I'd sing all the time, eyes closed and full of joy?

Would he fall in love with Momma again and ask her to marry him, and then my grandfather would see we were a normal, happy family after all?

My fingers itched to call in and speak to him for real. I had dialed the radio station's phone number so many times I had it memorized, but I never got up the nerve to press Call.

Because what would I say? "Hi, my name is Maybelle Dorothy Lane, and you're my daddy?"

No. It couldn't happen like that. What I needed was

some kind of a sign. A sign that my daddy wanted to know me as badly as I wanted to know him.

And maybe all that hope I put out into the universe worked some kind of magic, because my sign arrived the very next day.

* * + * *

It started with a special announcement.

"It's a big one, folks," my daddy said, his deep voice thrumming. "And I am *so* excited to share this news with you. Make sure to tune in next week, on the Fourth of July at seven p.m. We've got special programming that day to celebrate this wonderful country of ours, so my show will be running from seven to nine p.m. instead of my usual hours. So remember: tune in next week, July fourth, seven p.m. Trust me—you don't want to miss this. It's the biggest thing to happen to WKBC since . . . well"—he laughed his booming, sunshine laugh—"since *ever*. I hope you'll join me to hear what we've got cookin'."

I waited all week for his special announcement. I fidgeted. I watched TV, but I couldn't focus.

I could feel it. My daddy's announcement was going to be big.

A-sign-from-the-universe big.

Finally, the Fourth of July arrived.

The year before, we were still living in Baton Rouge and I'd spent the whole day at the pool with my best friend, Rosa. Then her older brother took us to the river to watch the fireworks shoot off from the big warship, the USS *Kidd*. I recorded each *pop* and *sizzle* and *bang* for my sound collection.

But this year, Momma and I didn't have anything special planned. The Pit Stop was throwing a party, which meant Momma had to work.

We had an early supper before she left for her shift, which was one of her last. She planned to spend most of the weekend getting all packed up and ready to drive to Miami, where her cruise ship was leaving from.

I had to pack, too. Gram had said she didn't think it was a good idea for her to come stay for that long. It didn't surprise me, given what had happened back in Baton Rouge, but it did make me sad. Now I was going to stay with Momma's friend Cynthia, and I was not looking forward to it. Her house smelled like nail polish, and it felt like she had a different boyfriend every week. The newest one's name was Wade. He rode dirt bikes and spat nasty brown juice into empty beer cans.

After Momma left, I did my chores. I pretended it wasn't the Fourth of July so I wouldn't miss Rosa and everything back in Baton Rouge quite so fiercely. Usually I didn't mind doing the dishes. It was all a part of my routine, which helped make the empty hours of my summer nights seem a little fuller.

But that evening, I couldn't pay attention to anything I was doing. The water was too hot, and I burned my fingers and kept dropping the soapy plates with a *clank* and even poked myself with the sharp tip of a knife.

Once I finished, I dried my hands and checked the cracked screen of my digital watch. It was only 6:11:04 p.m. How could I possibly wait a whole *hour* for the big special announcement?

I only had to think for a minute before I knew exactly how to distract myself: I would find a new sound to add to my collection.

So I went to the foot of the bed Momma and I shared and, from underneath it, took out my special shoebox.

It was full of tapes, all neatly labeled, as well as my tape recorder. It was an old-fashioned one that used real tapes, a little bit bigger than a deck of cards. I loved the cool weight of it in the palm of my hand. I had wanted it instead of the newer kinds you can plug into your computer, because I liked the idea that I could catalog and label each tape once I'd filled it up with sounds. Having the physical tapes made it feel official. Like I was a historian or something. A historian of sounds that most other people overlooked. I took the recorder out from the box and brushed my finger along its smooth plastic edge.

After setting my watch's beeping alarm for 6:55 *and* 6:59, I took my recorder outside and sat on the front step, not even sure what kind of sound I was looking for.

Mrs. Boggs, our neighbor and a teacher at my school, was sitting outside her RV. Her hair was pulled back into a tight bun, as always, but she had on clothes far more casual than she'd ever wear to school. Gray shorts, black T-shirt. I didn't think I'd ever seen Mrs. Boggs wear anything colorful. Her brown skin barely had a bead of sweat on it, whereas my usually pale white self was already lobster red and frizzy-haired. Maybe she had air-conditioning. Ours had broken the month before, and we couldn't afford to get it fixed.

She must have felt my eyes on her, because she looked up from her book and dipped her chin at me. "Miss Lane. Happy Fourth of July."

My stomach turned in the nervous way it always did whenever I had to interact with a teacher outside of school. I'd never had a class with Mrs. Boggs, and for that I was grateful. She taught remedial language arts, for the kids who struggled in normal classes. She was rumored to be the strictest teacher in our parish. Maybe in the entire state of Louisiana. In Pelican Park, Mrs. Boggs was the one who always went to knock on a front door when a party went too late or if music got too loud.

"The walls are thin, and there are children in this park who need to go to school in the morning!" I'd heard her holler more than once.

And you know what? Even adults listened to Mrs. Boggs, because, without fail, the parties broke up and the music always got lowered.

I gave a little wave back and, thankfully, she went right back to her book.

After that, I closed my eyes and tried to quiet down my mind. I've discovered that's the best way to really hear something. You've got to clear out all the junk that's swirling around your brain, like garbage in a river, before you can hear anything truly interesting.

I also tuned out the barking dogs, the TVs, and the thump of music from a couple trailers down. I sat for a while. I couldn't even say how long.

Then: *Shh-shhh-shhhkkkkk.*

I opened my eyes. I looked around.

Shh-shhh-shhhkkkkk, it went again.

A few paces in front of me, in the middle of the road, sat a fat green grasshopper.

When I got up to move closer, he hopped away. This happened a few more times until I was able to inch close enough to see what he was doing.

The noise came from his legs. Whenever he rubbed them together, it sounded like he was shaking a rain stick.

I set down my recorder gently, ever so gently, onto the

dirt road, and was so focused on not scaring the little bug away that I didn't notice the pounding footsteps.

Not until it was too late.

A cat tore by me, fur raised, yowling in anger.

I turned to see Jeremiah Johnson, Tommy and Jackson O'Brien, and two of the even younger O'Brien brothers running toward me like a pack of wild, snotty-nosed wolves. There were a few other cronies from Jeremiah's gang at school with them, too, but they were lagging farther behind. Tommy had an American flag tied around his neck, and it streamed out behind him like a cape. They were chasing that poor cat!

But as soon as Jeremiah noticed me, he grinned and changed course. Now he was running directly at *me*.

I jumped out of the way in the nick of time, tumbling into a ditch as they barreled on down the road, looking like a cartoon dust ball of fists and feet.

Once they'd passed, I scrambled to stand. None of them even glanced back to see if I was okay. The bug was long gone, and one of my elbows was scraped and stinging. My tape recorder was safe in my hand, but my radio—where was my radio?

That's when I saw it.

My beautiful vintage Gran Prix radio, lying there, covered in dust, with its wiry guts spilling out onto the road.

It was broken. Completely, utterly broken.

CHAPTER 5

"**N**O!" I screamed, falling to my knees. "No, no, no!"

"BOYS!" thundered Mrs. Boggs. She stood up, shut her book, and tucked it under her arm. "You all come back here at once."

Even though they were halfway down the road, they stopped at the sound of Mrs. Boggs's voice, their spines snapping straight. And, shockingly, they turned around and came back.

"Apologize to Maybelle this instant," Mrs. Boggs commanded. She wasn't even all that tall, but somehow she had the presence of a giant. She fixed her fiery stare on Jeremiah, who seemed to wilt under the heat of it. "All of you."

"Sorry, Maybelle," they all muttered. Even *Jeremiah*.

But "sorry" wasn't enough. "Sorry" wouldn't fix my radio.

"It's broken." I gathered up my poor radio and glared at the boys. "You ruined it!"

"Mr. O'Brien." Mrs. Boggs pointed at Tommy. "Try to help Maybelle fix her radio." Her voice softened a little. "I know you're good with things like that. And take that flag off from around your neck. Don't you know how disrespectful that is?"

"Yes, ma'am," Tommy said sheepishly. "Sorry, ma'am."

Tommy took the flag off, handed it to Mrs. Boggs, and then came over to me. He wiped sweat from his forehead, leaving behind a long streak of dirt. "Are you okay?"

He asked it in a low voice, like he didn't want anyone else to hear him. But he didn't have to worry, because the rest of his pack had already melted away.

I glared at him. "No, I'm not *okay!*"

"Mrs. Boggs is right. I'm good with fixing stuff; maybe I can help—"

A few hot tears fell onto my cheeks. "Haven't you done enough?"

The first alarm on my watch started to beep. Was it five to seven already? It couldn't be! "Oh no," I moaned, covering my face with my hands. "I'm going to miss it!"

Tommy pulled a Swiss Army knife out of his pocket and wiggled it. "Let me try? Please?"

I supposed he couldn't make it any *worse.* "F-fine."

Tommy unscrewed the plastic cover and got to work.

I checked my watch: 6:57. He was still working when my final alarm, for 6:59, went off.

"Are you almost done?"

"Yeah. Hold on."

The minute ticked over to 7:00, and he was still hunched over my radio. My beautiful vintage Gran Prix radio.

I was having trouble breathing. Speckles of light popped up around the edges of my vision. *Breathe, Maybelle,* I commanded myself. I couldn't have one of my attacks, not here, not now. I stared at a rock by the toe of my shoe and forced myself to focus on its details. It was light gray, about the size of a marble. It had crusted pale dirt on one side. It was a good stone to kick as you walked.

Somehow, focusing like this helped. The knot in my chest loosened just enough so I could glance up. Tommy was coaxing the wires back into the radio's plastic shell. Then he twisted the whole thing closed with the screwdriver on his Swiss Army knife. I held my breath as he pressed the On button.

The radio crackled to life.

"See?" He grinned. His blond hair was mussed, and he had streaks of dirt all over his face and shirt. "Good as new."

It sounded like it was playing from the bottom of a filled-up bathtub. That's another way to say it sounded *horrible.* It was not as good as new.

But in that moment, it didn't matter. I grabbed the radio from Tommy and pressed it against my ear.

"Time for our special Fourth of July announcement. In partnership with Bobby's Flamin' Hot Chicken, I'm very excited to announce that we're hosting our first annual Sing to Win singing competition!"

Tommy was staring at me. I turned my back on him.

"The prize is a *year's* supply of Bobby's Flamin' Hot Chicken and three dozen boxes of his famous Rockin' Ancho Chili Sauce. But that's not all. The competition will take place on July twentieth, here in our great country's Music City—Naaaaaaashville, Tennessee—and will be broadcast live across Tennessee, Mississippi, and Louisiana!"

He went on. "The judges' panel will be made up of radio DJs from a few different shows . . . and I am so pleased to tell y'all that *I* will be one of the judges. Yes, yours truly made the cut! The other fine ladies and gents I'll be sitting with are . . ."

I didn't listen to the rest. Only one thing was knocking around in my brain. His radio station was hosting a competition in Nashville. In two weeks.

And *he* would be on the judges' panel.

He would be there, in person, to judge the singers himself.

The next thing I knew, he was reading out the station's phone number, the one I already had memorized, and saying it was going to be competitive, so we had to act *fast*.

He finished by saying, "Good luck, faithful listeners, and happy Fourth of July. I hope to see your beautiful faces—and hear your beautiful voices—in Nashville, Tennessee. Now here's one of my favorites from Johnny Cash, to ease us into the show."

His words hung in the air around me, like gold-dusted magic. What were the odds my daddy was going to judge a singing competition *exactly* when Momma was out of town on a cruise ship?

This was my fate. My sign. It had finally arrived.

Without even knowing what I was doing, I sprinted toward our trailer.

"Hey! May!" Tommy called. "What's the matter? Where you going?"

Without answering him, I closed the door behind me so fast, it bounced back open. I didn't even bother to go back and push it closed. I didn't care if mosquitoes got in. I grabbed my old flip phone and started dialing.

It rang once. Twice. Three times. Had it rung a fourth time, I may have lost my nerve and hung up. But it didn't. A lady with a raspy voice answered.

"Hello, WKBC, Karleen speaking."

I opened my mouth, but nothing came out.

"Hello? Hello?" Karleen sounded real annoyed, like

she dealt with prank callers and time wasters every day. "I'm going to hang up if you don't answer. Three, two—"

My voice came out quieter than a mouse's squeak. "Wait."

"*Yes?*"

I could almost hear her tapping her foot. I cleared my throat. "I'd like to sign up. I mean, for the contest. To sing."

"Okay." I heard the rustling of paper. "Go ahead and sing something for me."

I swallowed. "You want me to . . . sing something? Now?"

There was a pause. "You're signing up for a singing competition, aren't you? Well, this is the first part of it. I need a sample. If you're any good, you can sing in Nashville. Now go on. Sing."

I was so taken aback that I didn't have time to be filled with nerves, like I usually was when it came to singing in front of other people. I just belted out a few lines of a song I'd heard on my daddy's show.

After I finished, Karleen was silent for a long minute. Then she laughed a phlegmy laugh, which quickly turned into a cough. "Huh. Well. That was unexpected. You got a set of pipes on you, I can tell you that much. You're in. Where you going to be coming in from?"

"Davenport, Louisiana."

"And what song do you plan to sing for the contest?"

I didn't have an answer for that. Karleen sighed and went right back to sounding annoyed. "Make sure you choose something soon and actually practice it," she grumbled. "If you need musical accompaniment, you'll have to provide it yourself. Nothing racy or provocative and no cussing. This will be broadcast live, remember. Best not make a fool of yourself." Karleen's voice suddenly turned sharp. "And one more thing . . . how old are you?"

Lie, my brain screamed. *Lie to her!*

But a lie is not what came out of my mouth. "I'm eleven. But I'll be twelve in December."

"Eleven, twelve, doesn't matter. All minors have to have a parent or guardian accompany them to the contest. There will be forms you'll need to fill out. Okay?"

"A parent?" I squeaked. "Forms?"

"Yes. Is that a problem?"

"No," I said quickly. I wouldn't focus on that right now. Like Momma always said, I'd cross that bridge when I came to it. "No problem."

"Good. Now write this down."

I searched the kitchen for a pen and piece of paper, but I couldn't find them. I was so scared the call might drop or that Karleen would get impatient and hang up on me that I just said, "I have a good memory. Tell me and I'll remember."

"We'll see you at four p.m. on July twentieth, at the Walk of Fame Park. Contest starts at five, so arrive at four. If you're late, you'll be disqualified. If you don't show, you're banned from all future WKBC 101.3 contests."

I repeated the details back to her, to make sure I had it all.

"That's right," she said. And then she hung up.

I don't know what I was thinking. I wasn't a spur-of-the-moment kind of person. I liked to collect sounds and listen to them, but *making* them? In public? That was a different story.

I wasn't nervous because I was bad. I knew I wasn't a bad singer. A voice deep inside told me I might even be a little bit *good*. Once, I sang a solo song for our school chorus in Baton Rouge that made my teacher cry. And every time Momma played her guitar, she tried to coax me into singing along.

But that was the old me. The Baton Rouge me. The Davenport me couldn't sing after everything that had happened. Not even with Momma. Not even by myself.

And now here I was, signed up to sing in a live radio contest, all the way in Nashville, a place I'd never been before. In front of a crowd of strangers.

In front of my daddy.

* ✳ ✣ ✳ ·

The next day, as Momma got packed and ready to go, I walked around like a zombie. I thought for sure she'd see it written across my face that I had a big secret burning brightly inside me.

"Is everything okay? Are you sick?" she kept asking me, holding her wrist against my forehead.

"I'm not sick. Everything's fine," I told her. "It's just so dang hot."

Momma frowned like she didn't quite believe me, but she kept on packing anyhow.

I still had to pack, too. Plus, I had absolutely no idea how I would get from Davenport all the way to Nashville for the contest. I'd have to do it in secret, because I was sure Cynthia would tattle on me to Momma the second she heard about my plans.

But it would work. It had to. The universe had given me the sign, so surely the universe would provide me a way to get there.

Then, the day before Momma was due to leave, the phone rang. I crossed my fingers that it was Jay, her boss at the auto shop, telling her she didn't have to come in for her last shift. I wanted to spend every minute I could with her before she left.

But it wasn't Jay. It was Cynthia.

"What? Oh no. But you—" Momma closed her eyes and rubbed her forehead slowly, the way adults do when they're disappointed. "No, I'm happy for you, but . . . no. You're right. You should definitely go. Don't worry about me. I'll figure it out. And, Cyn? Congratulations."

When Momma hung up, I made a *What was that about?* kind of face.

"You can't stay with Cynthia," Momma said, her voice flat. "Wade proposed, and they're going to Las Vegas to get married. They're already on their way there."

"Oh no," I said, and I meant it. For the first time since we'd found out Momma had gotten the job, I actually wanted her to go. It was the only way I'd even have a chance at getting up to Nashville.

"Then . . . will you stay here?"

Momma sighed. "No. I can't back out of my contract this late."

If I couldn't stay with Cynthia, where would I go? What would I do? Who would watch me for three whole weeks? "Then what will happen to me when you're gone?" I asked, my voice rising in panic. "You won't leave me here all alone, will you? You wouldn't do that, right? What if—"

She came over and took me gently by the shoulders. "Don't spiral, baby. Deep breaths. Relax your body. Remember what the doctor said? The more you relax, the more you breathe and let go of whatever you're worrying about, the better." Then she hugged me close.

Feeling her arms around me comforted me some, enough so that I could try my best to calm down. We sat there on the couch for a long time, breathing together. Finally, after what felt like an eternity of minutes, the worry pulled back a little. "I—I think I'm okay."

She tucked my hair behind my ears. "Good. That's good. Now listen to me. I promise you, if I can't find another good alternative for you—no, a *great* alternative— by the end of the day, I'll call the cruise company and drop out."

"But I thought it was too late."

Momma shrugged. "Even so, I'll still do it. I would never leave you all alone. Ever."

Hearing her say that made me feel a *little* better.

Momma glanced at the clock. If she was going to be on time for work, she should have left five minutes ago. "Are you sure you're okay? I can call Jay and tell him I'm not coming in—"

"No," I said firmly. I wouldn't let her get in trouble on account of me. "I'll be fine. You should go."

"Thank you," she said, kissing me on the head. I could tell she was relieved. I knew she wanted to keep on good terms with Jay, in case she needed the job at the auto shop when she got back from the cruise. Before she walked out the door, she turned around. "Don't worry, May. I'll figure out a solution while I'm at work. I'll be home by five, and we can talk more about it then. It will all work out. I promise."

"Okay," I said, but it came out shaky. Promises from Momma meant a lot to me. But for the first time maybe ever, I wasn't sure I believed her.

CHAPTER 6

When the door swung shut behind Momma, the silence was all I could hear. It rang. It shrieked.

Because that's the thing people don't realize about silence. It can be loud. The worst kind of loud. It can ring in your ears like a whine, reminding you that you're all alone. The whine was never so bad in Baton Rouge, but in Davenport, sometimes it was so strong it drowned out everything else.

Unlike most other kids on the planet, I wished summer vacation wasn't a thing. I'd rather be at school, even if it meant putting up with Jeremiah and his friends. I went to an after-school program that lasted until six, so during the school year, I was only home alone for a few hours at night while Momma was at the Pit Stop. I didn't want to tell Momma about how much I hated summer vacation, because I already knew she felt guilty she couldn't afford to put me in summer camp or anything like that.

A rumble of thunder and patter of rain was getting going, so I couldn't go outside to escape the silence of our trailer. I put on some music since my daddy's show wasn't on that day. Not because I wanted to listen to anything at the moment, really, but because I needed the company.

But it wasn't enough. I needed more. So I went and got my cell phone and flipped it open.

First I called my best friend, Rosa, who lived back in Baton Rouge. We mostly texted each other now, but I needed to hear her voice. I used to spend lots of afternoons at her house after school when Momma was working. The phone rang twice before Mrs. López picked up.

"¿Bueno?"

"Mrs. López," I said. "It's Maybelle. Is Rosa around?"

"Sí, Maybelle! One minute, okay? I will go check for her."

"Gracias," I replied.

Rosa's parents mostly spoke Spanish at home. I had picked up a lot of phrases and words just from being around their family. I used to be able to have whole conversations with Mrs. López in Spanish. And even if my accent was bad, she would smile and nod like I was doing it perfectly. But I was out of practice.

I heard the muffled sound of the phone being put down on the counter.

"Rosa!" Mrs. López called out. "Rosa, Maybelle está en el teléfono. ¿Quieres hablar con ella?"

"No!" Rosa shouted back in English. "Kylie's dad is picking me up to go to the pool any minute! Tell her I'll call her back."

I hung up before Mrs. López could pass the message along to me. I didn't want to hear the apology in her voice. Rosa and I had talked or texted every single day when I first moved, but now it was more like once every other week, and most of the time it was me reaching out to *her*. And the last few times I'd called, this same thing had happened—Rosa couldn't talk right then, but she promised to call me back later. Only, she didn't.

I could call Gram, I thought. To triple-check to make sure that she really couldn't stay with me.

My fingers hovered over the buttons. But then a tiny voice at the back of my head jabbed at me, like a red-hot poker. The last few times Gram and I had talked was because I'd called her—like with Rosa.

Then again, Gram and I were blood. I was her granddaughter. That had to mean something.

I bit my lip as I dialed her number and pressed Call. Because, like always, the loneliness won out.

But she didn't pick up.

I tossed the phone aside. I didn't know who else to try. Even Jeremiah Johnson always had a gang of people buzzing around him, and he was meaner than a rattlesnake.

Why did a boy like him get to have company, when I had to be alone?

This is why I'm going to Nashville, I reminded myself. To add someone to the short list of people I could call. And not any old kind of someone—someone amazing. Someone who would listen to me go on about my no-good, terrible day, really *listen,* and leave me smiling at the end of the conversation, like he did for that listener Shawna.

I needed him. I needed him to help drown out the silence.

· ＊ · ＋ ＊ ·

Momma got home a little after five, a triumphant smile on her face. "I've figured it out, May. I have the perfect solution."

I flipped my magazine shut. "What is it?"

Momma peeled off her work shirt before she came and joined me on the couch, wearing only her tank top. Even though she worked at the front desk and not in the garage, she was always embarrassed that she smelled like motor oil and gas after her shifts. But I only ever noticed her flowery shampoo.

"I can't believe I didn't think of it before. It's an even *better* solution than staying with Cynthia at her place. Are you ready for this?" She spread her hands out in front of her like she was about to announce a lottery winner. "Alice Boggs is going to watch you while I'm gone."

I stared at her. "Alice Boggs like Mrs. Boggs? The teacher Mrs. Boggs?"

"Yes." Momma's face crumpled a little. "Is that a bad thing? Are you okay with that?"

"It's not a bad thing," I said carefully. Because, honestly, it *did* make sense. At the beginning of the summer, Momma had instructed me that Mrs. Boggs was the adult I should go to if anything bad happened when I was home alone. And she'd gotten Jeremiah Johnson and the O'Brien boys to apologize to me, which was something I'd never thought would happen.

But Mrs. Boggs was also a *teacher.* At my school. It felt weird to be staying with a teacher outside of school. A super-strict teacher, at that.

"Will she have a lot of rules?" I asked.

Momma laughed. "I'm not sure. I don't think so. But if she does, try to go along with them, because Mrs. Boggs is an angel for agreeing to watch you for free. I tried to offer her some money, but she refused to take a penny."

"She did?"

Momma nodded. "She did."

Suddenly I realized how little I actually knew about Mrs. Boggs. For example, I had no idea her first name was Alice. I knew she was older than Momma but definitely much younger than Gram. She didn't smile very much, and she talked in a straight and level sort of way that made me doubt she was from Louisiana or anywhere else in the South, for that matter.

The one thing I *did* know about her was that she liked to read books over in Davenport Cemetery, which was right across the road from Pelican Park. It didn't seem to me like an entirely pleasant place to read, and yet Mrs. Boggs went over there most evenings.

She was an enigma, all right.

"Why?" I asked.

Momma cupped my cheek in her palm. "Probably because she knows you're such a good kid."

Was I? Did good kids lie to their mothers? Did good kids plan to run away to Nashville to meet their fathers? Did good kids feel this mixed up and lonely and angry all the time?

But I didn't say any of that. Instead, I leaned into Momma and let her stroke my hair. I would worry about the rest of it tomorrow.

* ✳ ✦ ✳ ·

The next morning arrived all too soon.

It had thundered and rumbled so loudly that I couldn't sleep. At some point, I slipped out of bed to sit by the open window and record the rolling booms of thunder and the constant pitter-patter percussion of rain against our thin roof.

I was still there by the window when Momma got out of bed, a little after six. She wasn't leaving until eight, but she wanted to make our "special occasion" pecan chocolate chip banana pancakes before she left.

When we sat down to eat, the pancakes felt like wet cement in my mouth. Momma kept squeezing my hand from across the table. She didn't eat much, either.

By seven-fifty-five, the trunk of the car was packed with Momma's bags, and her guitar was nestled in the back seat in its worn case.

Mrs. Boggs came out of her RV wearing a bathrobe, her hair all wrapped up in silk. She glanced at me and then at Momma. "I'll take good care of her, Gemma," she said. "I promise."

"Thank you *so* much," Momma said. "Really. I'm in your debt."

"Don't be silly. Now, if it's all right with you, I'm going to get a little more rest," Mrs. Boggs said. "Maybelle, why don't you come check in with me at nine-thirty?"

"Okay."

"Good. I'll see you then. Gemma, have a safe drive."

"Thank you again!" Momma called out. "From the bottom of my heart!"

After Mrs. Boggs had gone back inside her RV, Momma turned to me. "Like Alice said, check in with her as soon as she wakes up. I told her you might prefer to sleep at home instead of on her couch, so it's up to you."

"It is? Thank you," I breathed out. At least there was that.

Momma nodded. "I've made sure she's got all the important phone numbers. And this is for you." She peeled some rumpled bills from her wallet and handed them to me. "One hundred dollars. For emergencies only, May. I mean it. Stick it somewhere safe, okay?"

"Okay," I said, staring at the ground.

"Oh, May." She pulled me into a hug. "I'm going to miss you worse than all get-out."

"Then don't go," I whispered, but not loud enough for her to hear. Her long brown hair was still damp, and the smell of her flowery shampoo was stronger than ever.

I started crying. Momma started crying, too.

Eventually, she drew away from me. Her eyes were shiny and red. "You be good. Mind your manners. Don't forget to say your please-and-thank-you's. Be kind. Be courteous. I'll call you as soon as I get to Miami. I love you, Maybelle Lane."

And with that, she got into the car and drove away.

I ran behind her, getting sprayed by pebbles and pelted

by raindrops, all the way to the entrance of Pelican Park. She honked as she turned to the right and waved her hand out the window. I stood by the faded WELCOME sign and watched until the car was nothing but a distant speck on the road.

I watched until she disappeared and for a long while after that.

CHAPTER 7

After Momma left, I sat on the couch and watched the clock. The minutes ticked and tocked and drained away. Maybe Mrs. Boggs would sleep in until eleven or twelve today. Maybe even later than that. Maybe I wouldn't have to talk to her at all.

It wasn't that I didn't like Mrs. Boggs—I just didn't *know* Mrs. Boggs.

That's the funny thing about being alone so much. It makes you forget how to be with other people, even if that's the one thing you wish for more than anything in the world.

After a while, I ran out of minutes. Nine-thirty had arrived.

As I approached, I took in the details of her Winnebago like I was seeing it for the first time. It was the size of a bus, and it was mostly black, except for a swirling blue-and-white design down the side that reminded me of the Milky Way. Even though the wheels were sunk down into the mud, and the outside was coated in a thin layer of dust left streaked by the rain, it was still by far the nicest and most expensive-looking RV in all of Pelican Park. Honestly, other than the dirt and the dust, it looked almost brand-new. It must have cost a fortune.

And it was the only one here that actually looked *mobile*. Why was someone who could afford an RV like this living in a place like Pelican Park? If I were her, I would have left a long time ago.

The steps creaked beneath my feet. I counted to five-Mississippi. Ten. Finally, I knocked.

A few seconds later, the door swung open, and there stood Mrs. Boggs.

She'd changed out of her bathrobe into a gray T-shirt and dark jean shorts that went down to her knees, and her hair was pulled back. She had on a thin silver necklace with a diamond pendant that sparkled against her brown skin. I stared at it, wondering if it was real.

"Miss Lane," she said. "Good. You're punctual. I like that in a person. Come on in."

The door swung smoothly shut behind me as I followed her inside. I looked around, suddenly curious. I had never seen the inside of Mrs. Boggs's home. She never seemed to have any guests over, so I guessed not many people had.

The first thing I noticed was the books. Books were stacked in piles on the floor, on the kitchen counter, on the edge of the long leather sofa that was built into the opposite wall. Even more books lined some wooden shelves that had been built into the walls. I'd never seen so many books in all my life, not even at school. There were also lots of cardboard boxes stacked up against the walls and in the corners of the RV, which, if I had to guess, probably held even more books. It made some sort of sense, because Mrs. Boggs was a language arts teacher, after all, but wow.

The books and cardboard boxes made it feel cluttered, sure, but it was also *nice*. Like, really nice. The sky outside was still dark and gray from last night's storm, but inside Mrs. Boggs's RV, it was cozy and warmly lit. And it didn't feel like a motor home—it felt like a *home* home. There was art hung on the walls, and the floors were made of what looked like real wood, covered with soft rugs. There was even a dining table (also stacked with books), a small kitchen, and a hallway I guessed led to the bathroom and the bedroom.

Mrs. Boggs sat down on the leather sofa and looked up at me. "You weren't in my class this year, and I've never had you for a detention, have I?"

"No, ma'am."

I'd never had a detention, period. Though seeing how she'd handled Jeremiah and the O'Brien boys the other day, it didn't surprise me that Mrs. Boggs was the one who ran it.

"Then you don't know it yet, but you will: I like structure. Structure is important, even in the summertime. *Especially* in the summertime. I intend for you to respect the structure of my life. Can I count on you to do that?"

I nodded.

"Good. So here's the deal. During the school year I'm up most days before five, but in the summer, I let myself sleep until nine. Sometimes later. I expect you to check in with me at nine-thirty every day. We'll have lunch together at twelve-thirty, and then dinner at six sharp. I read and nap after lunch, so don't bother me between one and three unless something's on fire. I can make up the sofa if you'd like to stay here overnight, but your mom said you might prefer to sleep in your own bed, which is fine with me. Is all that clear?"

I nodded again. Somehow she'd managed to tell me all about her day and nothing about herself at the same time.

"What about the cemetery?" I blurted out before I could stop myself.

Mrs. Boggs's gaze sharpened. "What about it?"

"Well, I know you like to read over there. Don't you? But you didn't say anything about it in your list of rules."

"It's not a list of rules. It's the structure of my day. But I will give you one rule, if that's what you want: please respect my privacy."

"Okay," I said, feeling chided. My palms were starting to sweat from this encounter. "I'm sorry. I will."

Mrs. Boggs waved toward the front door. "All right. Off you go. The rain's stopped, so why don't you go get some fresh air before you come back here for lunch."

"I was going to have leftover pancakes. We still have a whole stack left."

Mrs. Boggs eyed me. "Fine. Today can be an exception." She got up, went over to the fridge, and took out an egg. She came over and handed it to me. "But please eat this, too. For protein. It's hard-boiled. Easiest way to peel it is in a bowl of cold water. Starting tomorrow, we'll have lunch together every day."

I took the egg from her, and before I could stop myself, I asked one last question. "Why'd you agree to watch me?"

Mrs. Boggs considered me for a moment. "Because it was the right thing to do. Now remember," she said, opening the door for me. "Dinner's at six. Don't be late."

· * · + * ·

I walked straight back home and plonked down onto the couch. The encounter had, for some strange reason, exhausted me.

Or maybe I was exhausted because I hadn't slept a wink the night before. Whatever the case, I only let myself lie there and recover for a couple of minutes. I knew I couldn't mope around all day. If I did, my heart would ache too much knowing Momma wouldn't be home tonight. She wouldn't be home for a long while. So I slid off the couch, went to the junk drawer in the kitchen, and opened it.

It was time to fix myself a plan.

From the drawer, I pulled out one of the creased paper maps of Davenport we used when we first moved to Pelican Park. Momma said it was easier for her to understand a place when she saw it on paper. She had learned the roads by now, but she held on to the maps just in case.

Which was lucky for me. I laid the map flat on the floor and found Pelican Park. Then I ran my finger to the left until I found what I was looking for. There. It looked to be about four miles to the west. The bus station.

Four miles there and four miles back was too far to walk, especially between the hours of one and three, Mrs. Boggs's napping hours.

What I needed was a bike.

There was one person in Pelican Park I knew who

had a bike, even if it was an old, rusty, low-riding one. Tommy O'Brien.

He liked to ride it back and forth and back and forth, again and again, along the single dirt road that went down the middle of Pelican Park, splitting the trailers on either side into two straight lines. One afternoon, I think I noticed him pass our trailer at least ten different times on that squeaking bicycle of his.

I hated the idea of asking a favor of him. Under normal circumstances, I'd rather walk to the moon than ask a favor of Tommy O'Brien. Especially after he'd ruined my radio. It hadn't been nearly the same since the boys had run it over, and Saturday it died about halfway through my daddy's show. If I had it my way, I'd never see Tommy's sweaty, dirt-streaked face ever again. Or at least not until school started.

But this was different. This was necessary.

The sounds of Tommy's mother hollering and a baby crying rang out across their patchy bit of yard as I approached. The rain had stopped, but the sky was still a steely, threatening gray. As I came closer, I heard feet scuffling inside the trailer and more shouting. I was about to lose my nerve and turn around when the front door banged open.

"Oh, would you look who it is. *May's* come to see you!" Jackson shouted, pulling Tommy into a headlock.

Tommy managed to fight him off, but when he stood up, his blond hair was mussed and his face was bright red.

Even though Jackson was in the grade below us at school, he towered over Tommy by about five inches. At least Jeremiah wasn't with them today.

Tommy stared at me. "What do *you* want?"

"Uh," I said. To be honest, I was completely taken aback. His voice was way different than it was when he was trying to fix my radio on Friday. "I was wondering—"

"We can't hear you!" Jackson shouted in a singsongy voice.

I cleared my throat and tried again, focusing on the tips of Tommy's scuffed-up sneakers. "I was wondering if I might be able to borrow your bike for a couple of hours. Please." Then I raised my gaze and stared at him, trying to mimic Mrs. Boggs's imposing presence. "I figure it's the least you can do, after you ruined my radio."

"No," Tommy said quickly. His face was still beet red. He shot a look at Jackson, who was smirking at me. "You can't. And I didn't ruin your radio. I was trying to help you fix it. Go away!"

Now it was my turn to blush. He didn't even consider it. I spun around and ran off without saying another word. Jackson's laughter trailed after me like a swarm of stinging bees.

Ten minutes later, though, there was a knock at my front door. It was Tommy, and he had his bike with him.

"Here," he said, thrusting it forward. He kept looking over his shoulder. "I'm sorry about before. You can use it for as long as you like. Leave it out front when you're done. You don't have to knock or anything."

Before I could say a word, Tommy turned on his heel and took off. I watched him go, my mouth hanging open.

"Boys," I muttered to myself.

I didn't think much longer about his strange behavior. I had places to be.

* * * * *

The ride to the bus station was about as pleasant as swallowing a bucketful of swamp water. There were big puddles from the storm all along the road, and even though cars slowed down to pass me, their tires still sprayed me from top to bottom with muddy water.

Tommy's bike squeaked and shrieked the whole way there. The steering was so ornery that I almost feared the bike would buck me off and ride away without me.

By the time I arrived at the station, I was out of breath, sopping wet, and half-crazed from the squeaking of the brakes. It had taken me almost a full hour to bike the four miles, and after I bought my ticket, I would have to turn around and bike right back.

As I waited in line, I kept checking and rechecking that the cash from Momma was still safe and dry in my pocket. Hopefully this wasn't a big mistake. She hadn't even been gone a full day, and here I was, planning to use her emergency money for a bus ticket to Tennessee.

I kept reminding myself that the chances to meet my daddy were few and far between. It had to be fate.

Didn't it?

But as the line grew shorter, I grew less and less certain about my plan. There were so many things that could go wrong. What if an actual emergency happened, and I needed this money? Or what if my daddy got real angry with Momma that she never told him about me? Could he get the law involved? The last thing I wanted to do was get Momma in any kind of trouble.

Or—and my stomach churned the worst at this— what if my daddy *didn't* want to find out he had a daughter? What if he preferred his childless life as it was, and knowing I existed went and messed everything up for him?

And then, of course, as the final nail in the coffin of my doubts: the singing. Was I really, truly prepared to get up on a stage in front of a crowd of people and *sing*? The last time I sang was a disaster.

Someone bumped into me hard, from behind. I rubbed my shoulder and turned around. "Hey! Watch where you're going."

It was a teenage boy with messy red hair. "Sorry," he muttered before ambling away.

"Next," came a bored-sounding voice from the window.

I looked around. Somehow, I was the next one in line. I stepped forward to the counter.

"I'd like a ticket to Nashville, please," I told her. "For the twentieth of July."

The lady didn't look up at me or ask my age. She just *clicker-clack*ed away on her computer. "I've got a night bus on July nineteenth, eight-oh-five, transfer in Jackson and Memphis. It'll get you into Nashville at eight-oh-seven the next morning. Sixty-five fifty-one, one-way."

Sixty-five dollars? I didn't realize it was going to be so expensive. I'd never been out of Louisiana before. I wouldn't have enough money to get back if this all went wrong.

Maybe my daddy would pay for the bus ride back. Heck, maybe he would want to drive me himself. We could talk and listen to music and get to know each other. Maybe we could stop for french fries and milkshakes along the way.

"Miss?" the lady said. She sounded impatient. "Hello?"

I took a deep breath. This was it. I was ready to jump.

"I'll take it," I said. I reached into my pocket.

Oh *no*.

I frantically patted this way and that way, but the pocket was empty. *All* of my pockets were empty.

No, no, no.

Momma's emergency money was gone!

CHAPTER 8

I searched all over the bus station for the teenage boy with the red hair, but he was gone. Long gone. I knew it had to be him once I replayed it in my head. He had probably watched me check on the money in my pocket again and again. I was what a TV detective would call an easy mark.

How could I have been so stupid?

I knew I couldn't report him, either. Because if I did, a police officer would ask why a young girl tried to buy a bus ticket all alone. I couldn't begin to imagine the look on Mrs. Boggs's face if a police officer came knocking on her door the first day of Momma's absence, dragging me along by the ear.

I left Tommy's bike in a heap on his front lawn.

For the rest of the day, I lay on the couch and stared at the ceiling.

Sure, I was petrified about singing, but deep down, an electric current of desire to finally meet my daddy was flowing through my whole body. I wanted to meet him so badly, the entire trailer seemed lit up with it.

Momma always said me and her were like two peas in a pod. I thought so, too, but she was gone a lot. Usually I was alone in our pod. Maybelle, the solo pea. But since I'd started listening to my daddy's show, I'd kept track of all the things we had in common. His silly sense of humor and the kinds of things that made him laugh. How he liked to drink water without any ice. The funny way he pronounced "room," just like me. And those things were from only a few hours of listening.

What if me and my daddy had a lot more in common? What if we were *also* like two peas in a pod?

But now I had no money. No ticket. No plan. And no one to help me.

* ✳ ˙ ₊ ✳ ˙

"Punctual again," Mrs. Boggs said when I knocked on her door for supper at six o'clock. She was holding a wicker basket that had a pair of dirty gloves and clippers in it. "That's good. Follow me. You can help me in the garden."

I followed her around back to a little patch of muddy yard. A single lawn chair with fraying plastic straps sat next to a few rows of raised garden beds. Plants grew up and out, this way and that way, like a tangled slice of jungle.

"We need to gather about three cups' worth of okra. That's this plant. Only look for the pods that are about two to three inches in length. If they don't snap easily," she said, tugging on one, "they're too mature, too fibrous. It would be like chewing on shoelaces. Got it?"

I nodded.

"Good." She pointed at the gloves in the basket. "And wear these to protect your skin."

We both got started on the okra picking, me with the gloves and Mrs. Boggs with her bare hands. The pods made a strange, popping *snap, snap, snap* as I took them off the stalk. It was soothing. If I was to do this again, I would have to remember to bring my tape recorder.

"Don't you need gloves?" I asked her after a few minutes.

"I only have the one pair. But don't worry," she said. "I'm good at this. And I'd rather you have them."

That small bit of kindness was enough to shake something loose in me.

I managed to hide the first couple of tears and sniffles from Mrs. Boggs. She'd moved around to the other side of the raised garden bed, and the okra's thick leaves hid my face from her.

But by the time she'd ushered me inside her Winne-bago and had added the okra to a bubbling pot, the tears were streaming down my face.

Soon enough, I hiccupped a sob.

"I know you're homesick for your mom," Mrs. Boggs said, shaking some salt into the pot. "But she'll be home soon enough, and you won't have to put up with my company for too much longer."

"N-no." I hiccupped again and wiped the tears from my cheeks. "It's not that."

Mrs. Boggs stopped stirring and looked over at me. "Oh? Then what is it?"

"It's nothing."

"I don't believe you. Out with it. The truth."

She crossed her arms like she meant business, but there it was again—that kind look in her eyes.

"I— There's this contest," I said, trying unsuccessfully to stop crying. "A singing contest, all the way up in Nash-ville. I signed up as a contestant, and I want to go with my whole heart, but I've got no way to get there anymore."

Mrs. Boggs's eyes flashed, sharper than a hawk's. "What do you mean, no way to get there *anymore*? How were you planning to get there in the first place?"

The thing about keeping everything on the inside is that it builds and builds and builds, and you can never be too sure when it will all come pouring out. Or to who.

Because even though I knew it was a terrible idea, I

told Mrs. Boggs almost everything. I told her about my trip to the bus station earlier, and about how the red-haired boy had stolen Momma's emergency money from my pocket without me even noticing.

"You should never have left Pelican Park today, Maybelle. You could have been hurt."

"But you never said I had to stay in Pelican Park while you were napping."

"Because you seem like a smart girl, and I thought it was a given." Mrs. Boggs turned and started stirring the pot again. The wooden spoon clanked against the side, and bits of tomato flew up out of the pot. "And you were planning to go up to Tennessee without as much as a peep to me, is that right?"

"I'm sorry," I said. And then the reality of what I'd told her came crashing down onto me. "I shouldn't have done it. Please don't tell."

"Seeing as you broke my trust on the very first day, you'll be sleeping here tonight so I can keep an eye on you. Understand?"

I nodded.

Mrs. Boggs didn't say anything else for a long time. I was about to start sweating bullets when, finally, she spoke.

"Do you like it spicy?"

"What?"

Mrs. Boggs pointed at the pot with her spoon. "I said, do you like it spicy?"

"Oh. Yes. Yes, ma'am."

"Good. Dinner will be ready in five minutes. Go on and move some of those books off the table. Silverware's in the drawer to my left."

Mrs. Boggs didn't say anything about my confession for the rest of the night. Not one single word about it. In fact, we barely spoke at all.

CHAPTER 9

I had trouble sleeping that night. I tossed and turned on Mrs. Boggs's couch, my legs getting all tangled up in the unfamiliar blankets. And the later it got, the more my worry grew.

What on earth had I been thinking, telling Mrs. Boggs all that? Would she call Momma first thing and tell her what I'd done? I didn't know what would be worse—getting in trouble, or having Momma be disappointed in me. Every time I was close to actually falling asleep, my eyes would snap open and the dread would surge in all over again.

What was wrong with me? I was usually so good at keeping my sad and bad feelings hidden on the inside. And then, with the tiniest little push, I had gone and told Mrs. Boggs almost everything.

At least I had the good sense not to mention that my

daddy was one of the judges. If Mrs. Boggs planned to call Momma and tell her what I'd done, I couldn't bear the idea of Momma on the phone in some hotel room, knowing just how much I'd lied to her *and* lost her emergency money.

The next morning, I woke to the sun streaming in through the RV windows. I sat up. "Mrs. Boggs?"

"Outside," she called back.

As I folded the blankets, I formed my plan. I would go out there and immediately tell her I made the whole thing up. That I lied to cover up how sad I was that Momma was gone.

When I got outside, she was standing by the back of the Winnebago with some kind of a floppy book in her hands. She seemed to be inspecting one of the back wheels.

She glanced over her shoulder at the sound of my footsteps. "Good morning, Maybelle."

I cleared my throat, ready to start my story. But before I could say a word, Mrs. Boggs snapped the book shut and turned to face me.

"I spoke to Darryl last night, and for whatever reason, he seems to think I should help you," she said. "I'd like to maintain the same structure on the road as I do here. Since I like to sleep until nine, we probably won't be on the road most days until ten or so. I feel comfortable driving about two to three hours a day, and I'd like to make some stops along the way, so that means it should take us about five or six days to get there."

Now I was confused. What on earth was she talking about? "I don't think I understand. Get where?"

"To Nashville," Mrs. Boggs said, like it was the most obvious thing in the world. "For your contest."

I felt the urge to clean out my ears with my fingers, like they do in cartoons, to make sure I wasn't hearing things. I looked between her and the Winnebago. "You mean . . . you don't mean to say that *you* intend to drive me there, do you?"

"That's exactly what I mean to say."

I couldn't believe it. *Mrs. Boggs* was going to take me to Nashville?

And just like that, the little bird inside my soul woke up and started to sing again.

"Before we leave, I want you to call your mom and make sure she's okay with us taking this little road trip. If she's uncomfortable with it, we don't go. Is that clear?"

"Yes!" I cried. "Yes, yes, I will! Oh, thank you, ma'am, thank you so much. I don't believe it!"

I don't know what came over me, but I ran right on over to Mrs. Boggs and threw my arms around her. She stood there with her arms at her sides as I hugged her, stiffer than a plywood board.

"All right," she said. "Go make that call. I'll need a few

days to check the systems. I haven't taken this gal any-where in a long time, so I have to make sure it's in good working order. What day is the contest again?"

"July twentieth," I told her. The date sparkled in my mind, bigger and more important than my birthday, or any other holiday, for that matter.

"Good," Mrs. Boggs said. "If we aim to leave by the end of the week, we'll still have time to get up there with-out having to hurry."

I think I floated back to my trailer. I'm pretty sure if there was a video recording of me, my feet wouldn't be touching the ground. All I could think was that I had to find whoever this Darryl was who had talked Mrs. Boggs into helping me and give him a quart-size jar of Mom-ma's famous candied pecans as my thanks.

But as soon as I got inside and took stock of my situa-tion, I came plonking back down to earth.

First things first: I had to call Momma. I couldn't tell her the full truth. I couldn't tell her that I was going to Nashville to meet my daddy. I thought of all the things she said in the car ride to the Shop 'n Save earlier that summer. *He'll only break your heart.* She'd never allow me to go if she knew the full truth.

So I picked up the phone, and as it rang, I asked for God's forgiveness for what I was about to say.

* ✳ ✦ ✳ ·

I lied to Momma. *Again.*

It wasn't exactly a plain-as-day lie, it was more that I didn't tell her the whole truth of the situation. I told her I signed myself up for a singing contest in Nashville, which was true, and that Mrs. Boggs had offered to drive me up there if Momma was okay with it, which was also true.

But I didn't tell her the contest was being put on by a radio station. And I *definitely* didn't tell her my daddy was one of the judges.

"One of my friends from school told me about it," I lied.

She was so distracted by the word "friend" that she ignored everything else. "A friend? A *new* friend? From school?"

The excitement in her voice made me cringe. "Yeah. Her name's, um, Sarah. So can I go?"

"Yes! Oh, yes, yes, yes, you can go! I'm so proud of you, May. I know you haven't been much in the mood to sing recently, but no one's got a voice like yours. You'll win that contest. I *know* you will. I have faith in you."

We talked a little bit more, but I was almost relieved when Momma said she had to go to a crew-training session down in the lobby of her hotel.

"Love you more than all the orange candies in the whole world, May," Momma said. "And I'm so proud of you. Please make sure to thank Alice for me, a million times over, and tell her to call me if she needs anything."

"I will." As soon as I hung up the phone, I shoved my guilty feelings down as deep as I could. I even let myself smile.

Because it was happening. I didn't have to take a bus. I didn't have to hitchhike or lie about my whereabouts or sneak out of Pelican Park in the dead of night. I was going to Nashville. I was going to meet my father. I squealed into my fists and did a cartwheel, right there in our cramped living room.

• ✳ ˙ ₊ ✳ •

The next few days inched slowly forward, minute by minute. My focus had disappeared entirely, so the normal things I'd do to pass the time—add sounds to my collection, watch TV, read magazines, listen to music or my daddy's show—couldn't keep my brain occupied. All I could do was jitter and pace, pack my overnight bag, empty it out, and repack it.

Finally, Mrs. Boggs announced at lunch that she'd be ready to go the next morning. I had gone back to my trailer and was triple-checking my packing job when there was a *knock-knock-knock*ing at the door. I swallowed, suddenly nervous it was Mrs. Boggs here to tell me that the whole thing was actually a bad idea, and that we couldn't go after all.

Thankfully, it wasn't Mrs. Boggs. It was Tommy

O'Brien. He had on the same shirt he'd been wearing the last few times I'd seen him, but it was inside out and backward. A big, mean-looking bruise was starting to bloom on his left cheek.

I eyed him. "Hey, Tommy. You want something?"

"Hey. I was checking . . . I never checked to make sure that everything was okay the other day. You know, with my bike."

"Oh. Yeah," I said. "I left it in front of your place. Didn't you see?"

"Yeah, no, I saw it." Tommy scuffed the ground with his shoe. "I was wondering if the, uh, brakes were okay. They've been acting up."

I shrugged. "They were fine. A little squeaky. No. Actually, they were a lot squeaky."

Tommy rubbed the back of his neck. "Yeah, I got to fix that. You can borrow it again if you want. You need it for anything else?"

"No," I said. The excitement of the last few days bubbled right back up inside me like I was a shook-up can of soda pop. "I don't need it because Mrs. Boggs and I are leaving tomorrow. We're going on a road trip in her Winnebago."

"You're going somewhere? With . . . Mrs. Boggs? Just the two of you?"

"Yep."

Tommy's expression darkened. "Why *you*?"

"What's that supposed to mean?"

"You weren't even in her class. She barely knows you. It's weird. But whatever," he muttered. "Doesn't matter."

I put my hands on my hips. "Can I help you with anything else?"

"No."

"Good. See you."

I didn't mean to *slam* the door in his face, not exactly. But since our door sticks in the heat, you really had to shove it in there.

I went over to Mrs. Boggs's for supper at six o'clock sharp, same as always. I was starting to understand why she liked her days so structured. It was kind of soothing, knowing what to expect and exactly when to expect it.

And same as the days before, she was waiting for me by the steps with a wicker basket and some clippers. But instead of going around back to her garden, we went down the dirt road to the grassy field separating Pelican Park from the swamp.

"We're going to gather some wildflowers," she instructed me. "As many as we can find."

And so we did. Once I had waded through the field's long, scratchy grass, filling up the basket with as many of the delicate yellow flowers as I could find, I headed back to where Mrs. Boggs was picking flowers and handed her my bunch. "Who are they for?"

She inspected the flowers. She pulled out a few wilted ones and tossed them onto the ground. "They're for Darryl."

I perked up at that. The mysterious Darryl. The person who'd talked Mrs. Boggs into taking me to Nashville. I'd never noticed Mrs. Boggs welcoming company into her RV, but if we were going to give flowers to a person named Darryl, then it meant she had to have at least one friend around here. And I had to thank him. "Can I come with you when you give them to him? I'd like to give him my regards."

Mrs. Boggs gave me a long look. "If you want. We can go see him after dinner."

She made collard greens with bacon fat and red beans for supper. She spent most of the time ignoring me and her plate of food as she clicked away on her slender laptop. It was less than half the size of the clunker Momma and I had.

"What are you doing?" I asked.

"Mapping out our route," Mrs. Boggs said. She seemed lost in thought, so I didn't bother her again. It wasn't that hard—I'd grown used to the silence of eating alone. Plus, the beans were so good, I ate three big bowlfuls.

Once the washing up was done, Mrs. Boggs gathered the flowers in her arms. "Ready?"

I didn't realize where we were going until we had

already crossed the road. The sun had just set, casting the world in a gloomy purple light, like the color of an old bruise. I felt like a fool for not understanding earlier.

As we walked through the cemetery entrance, I stayed as close to Mrs. Boggs as possible. I had never had the guts to go explore the cemetery on my own.

"Do you mind?" Mrs. Boggs said when I stepped on the heel of her shoe for the third time. "I could use a little breathing room."

"Sorry."

The cemetery was surrounded by a low chain-link fence. It had bowed inward in a few places, and other spots were sharp and rusty. We walked past rows and rows of crumbling gravestones and raised crypts made of cracked concrete, most of which were overrun with weeds. The grass was patchy with mud in some places and overgrown in others. The few trees dotting the cemetery were covered with Spanish moss, which hung down from the branches like strands of spiderwebs. I couldn't shake the feeling that someone was right behind me.

After we passed a few more rows, Mrs. Boggs stopped walking and bent down, dusting off leaves from a headstone in front of us.

I have to say, I was surprised by this grave, given the state of the rest of Davenport Cemetery. There were fresh flowers growing at the headstone's base, and the grass all around it was a bright, healthy green, and neatly trimmed.

The headstone—which still looked pretty new—said:

HERE LIES DARRYL BOGGS,
WHO WAS LOVED.

When I looked up, Mrs. Boggs was staring at me. "You said you wanted to give your regards. Go on, then."

I cleared my throat and turned to face Darryl. I wasn't sure exactly what to say, as I had never spoken to a gravestone before. "Well, thank you, Darryl," I said stiffly. I cleared my throat again. "I do appreciate your wise counsel to Mrs. Boggs. Well, that's all. Goodbye."

I looked at Mrs. Boggs. She gave me a tight nod and waved me off. "Good enough. Now go on and give us some privacy, please."

I went over and sat down against the base of a sweet gum tree while Mrs. Boggs paid her own respects. I could tell Mrs. Boggs would have preferred I went farther, but I was too scared to go more than ten paces away. From the corner of my eye, I saw her sink down onto her knees and carefully arrange the flowers we picked together beneath the word LOVED.

"Hello, darling," I heard her say. "How is my sweet,

handsome husband tonight? I'm fine, fine," she went on. "I did that online exercise class I was telling you about, but now my left knee's acting up again. I know you'd tell me to stretch more. This morning, I—"

I only listened for a few more seconds before I turned away and started humming to myself.

Because, as curious as I was about Mrs. Boggs, even *I* understood that some conversations were too private to be eavesdropped upon.

CHAPTER 10

We left Pelican Park the next day three hours behind schedule. Mrs. Boggs had wanted to leave by ten in the morning, but it was nearing one p.m. by the time we were all packed up and ready to go.

Even though we were late getting going, it still felt like a miracle. I was for sure expecting a road bump. A popped tire or a bad engine. Momma and I always had car trouble, so I assumed other people did, too.

But when Mrs. Boggs stuck the key in the ignition, the Winnebago roared to life like a jet plane, the copilot seat vibrating beneath me.

"Ready?" she asked.

I clutched my half-full bag of Tootsie Pops, the special snack I had chosen on my last trip to the Shop 'n Save with Momma. "Yes ma'am!"

The RV lumbered down Pelican Park's bumpy dirt road, and as it did, stacks of Mrs. Boggs's books fell down onto the floor.

"Shoot," she said, checking over her shoulder. "We'll have to do something about that."

We passed by the O'Briens' trailer. Jackson was sitting on his little brother Bobby, rubbing dirt in his face as Bobby tried to squirm free. Tommy's bike was propped against the trailer's side, but I didn't see him anywhere.

I held my breath as we approached Pelican Park's exit. The turn signal clicked. We took a right onto the paved road, and just like that, we were on our way. No one came out to stop us. No one put up a gate or came chasing us down.

We were free.

"We'll go up through Mississippi and then through Memphis," Mrs. Boggs told me. "It should take between five and six days, but I've left us a whole week because I might need an extra day here or there to recuperate from all this driving. Darryl was the one who liked to drive this thing, not me. We've got the time, though, so don't worry. And if we get there early, we can explore Nashville."

I kept my eyes glued to the window as the world rushed by around us. Though, to be honest, it was more like the world was *creeping by* around us, because Mrs. Boggs drove slower than molasses.

Lumbering along was okay with me, though, because it gave me more time to look around. The interstate we were driving on was raised up on thick concrete stilts, and we passed over wide stretches of brown water, dotted here and there with boggy green islands.

After about an hour, a sign appeared on the side of the interstate that said NEW ORLEANS, 112 MILES.

I held my breath as I watched it pass.

I turned to Mrs. Boggs. "Are we going through New Orleans?"

"No. It's out of the way. Maybe on the way back." She glanced at me. "Why?"

"No reason." I had only been to New Orleans once, less than a year earlier. And I would never forget that visit for as long as I lived. I fidgeted for a second with the wrapper of a brown Tootsie Pop before asking the question I was really wondering about. "Mrs. Boggs, do you believe in magic?"

She considered my question. "Well, it depends. What exactly do you mean by 'magic'? Storybook magic, like wizards and potions and things like that?"

"No," I said. "Not *magic* magic. Quieter than that. Magic more like . . . something in the real world you can't quite explain."

"Ah. I see what you're getting at," Mrs. Boggs said, nodding. She stayed quiet for a long minute. Finally, she said, "I'm not sure what I think. Darryl thought science was a certain kind of magic. Stars, black holes, the Big Bang, the genesis of life itself—all of it. And then in college, I learned all about Jewish mysticism from one of my favorite professors. She said there's magic and power in numbers, and in giving things names. But if I'm being honest, I'd say no. I don't believe in magic, storybook or otherwise. Though I suppose my answer might have been different had you asked me a couple years ago."

"How come?"

"Because things happen in life, and they change you," Mrs. Boggs replied. "Now, why are you asking me about magic?"

I squirmed a little in my seat. Even though I'd brought it up, I suddenly realized it was too complicated to explain. And I knew it'd come out jumbled and messed up if I tried to say it out loud. So I shrugged and turned toward the window. "No reason."

We settled back into silence. But of course, I did have a reason. I asked about magic because I believed in it.

And I believed in it because I saw it for myself, that night with Momma in New Orleans, and I would never forget it for as long as I lived.

We'd gone for the blues. It was right after we moved to Davenport, and we were having car trouble, so Momma and I had to take a few different buses to get to New Orleans. We were going to try and see Moony Phil and the Porchrockers, a band that Momma loved almost as much as she loved John Lee Hooker and the other "greats," as she called them. They were playing in a restaurant attached to a fancy hotel.

We couldn't afford tickets to the show, so we snuck in through a door in the back alley leading into the restaurant's steamy kitchen. We didn't get more than a couple of feet before we were stopped by an enormous chef, as fearsome in his stained white apron as a hungry polar bear.

"Are you trying to sneak in?" he roared, waving his axe-size knife in the air. "Go on, get out of here!"

I turned on my heel to get out of there, but Momma grabbed my arm and stopped me. Then she looked that scary chef right in the eye and said one single word.

"Please."

She had barely spoken louder than a whisper, but the power she put behind that tiny little word made my hair fly back.

She said it in a way that was like staying to hear the music was the only thing she had ever wanted in her whole entire life, and she stuffed all that meaning into one single itty-bitty pint-size word.

Please.

It felt like the whole room fell silent. Even the dinging of pots and pans and the hiss of the stove seemed to quiet down to listen to Momma's plea.

It was like magic. No—it *was* magic.

"Please," she said again. Even quieter this time.

Suddenly the big chef wasn't nearly so scary. His whole face softened, he was so entranced by Momma's small bit of word magic. He let us through, and even sent out a basket of donuts he said were "on the house," still hot from the fryer and covered in a snowy dusting of powdered sugar.

Momma spent the whole show acting like we were at church and it was God himself onstage, strumming his blues guitar. I liked the music, and I even recorded one little bit with jazzy notes like a hammer jumping up a ladder, even though signs on the black velvet walls all screamed NO VIDEO, NO RECORDING! in bright red lettering.

But mostly I practiced Momma's magic beneath my breath, because I sure wanted to learn how to squish up all my deepest hopes and yearnings and stuff them into one tiny little word, like Momma had.

"Please," I whispered to myself as the deep, sad notes of Moony Phil's saxophone filled the room. "Please."

CHAPTER 11

We finally stopped after three long hours of driving so Mrs. Boggs could take her afternoon rest. We were still an hour outside of Baton Rouge, which was difficult to believe. The drive from Davenport to Baton Rouge should have only taken two hours *total*. At this rate, I figured my twelfth birthday would come and go by the time we arrived in Nashville.

"I'd rather be safe than sorry," Mrs. Boggs kept telling me as cars laid on their horns and flew by us. "Because have you seen the size of this thing? It's like a bus on steroids. A battering ram. So I'm going to drive it with caution and respect."

As soon as Mrs. Boggs pulled the RV off into a rest area and put it in park, I leapt from my seat and dashed right to the bathroom. I was too nervous to stand up while we were driving, so I'd been holding it the whole time, and now I *really* had to go.

But the door wouldn't open.

I rattled the handle. "It's locked, I think."

Mrs. Boggs was already in her bedroom. "Use your elbow to pop the lock open," she called out from behind the closed door. "Sometimes it gets jammed."

So I did. The door popped open. And then I screamed.

Because the bathroom wasn't empty. There was already somebody inside. Tommy O'Brien was asleep on the floor, with an old, dirty duffel bag as his pillow.

As soon as I screamed, he jolted awake.

"Hey, May," he said, rubbing his eyes. "Surprise?"

"Tommy O'Brien. What are you doing here?"

"I thought I'd come along."

I stared down at him. "You can't come. No way."

He frowned. The bruise on his cheek was much darker today, and his eye was a little swollen from it. "You don't have to be mad. She was *my* teacher, not yours. That's got to count for something. I like adventures, too, you know."

Tommy and his group at school had spent the last year making my life miserable, and now he was trying to glom on to *my* road trip? Now we'd have to turn around and drop him back off, and it would throw us behind schedule by a whole day!

"This is one of the stupidest things you've ever done,

Tommy O'Brien," I said through clenched teeth. "And for you, that's really saying something."

"Why are you making so much noise out there?" Mrs. Boggs said, coming out from her bedroom. "I'm trying to— Oh," she said when she saw Tommy. "Oh my. It appears we have a stowaway. What are you doing here, Mr. O'Brien?"

"May said you were going on a road trip. And . . . I was thinking . . . hoping maybe I could come with y'all. Please? Please let me come? I even brought a sleeping bag and everything." He wiggled his duffel bag in the air.

Yeah, right, I wanted to say. *As if.*

But when I glanced at Mrs. Boggs's face, it looked as though she might *actually* be considering it. Then she said, "Well, I suppose one more couldn't hurt. We'll have to call your dad first, to make sure it's okay."

No, I thought. Absolutely not. Tommy could *not* come. "Can I talk to you, please?" I asked Mrs. Boggs. "In private?"

Tommy waited inside while I went to talk some sense into Mrs. Boggs in the parking lot. "He can't come. No way. He'll ruin everything!"

"I don't know about that," Mrs. Boggs said. "Maybe you're being a little too harsh."

"Him and his friends, they . . ." I trailed off. It wasn't like they'd stuck my head in the toilet or beat me up or done anything big or obvious like that. It was the little things. The looks, the small comments, the whispers and laughter behind my back. The way they made me feel separate from everyone else at school. How could I explain *that*? "They're awful, that's all. Please don't let him come."

"Some of those boys he hangs out with really are no good. I'll give you that," Mrs. Boggs said. "I know, because most of them are in my class, and all of them have spent time with me in detention. But Tommy's different. He's a good boy hanging with the wrong crowd. I need you to give him a chance."

It was true that Tommy was never the ringleader. But did that matter? He still hung out with Jeremiah. In fact, Tommy trailed him around school like a shadow. Even if he stayed quiet while Jeremiah whipped his mean words at me, his silence still spoke volumes. It said that it was all okay. That the way Jeremiah treated me was fine.

What if I did a terrible job singing—or worse yet, got up onstage and *froze*—and Tommy went and reported every detail to Jeremiah? All of this was hard enough as it was. I didn't need one of Jeremiah's minions spying on me, too. "I can't. I just can't. And I swear to you right now, Mrs. Boggs, if you let him come, I won't say a single word to him the entire time. I won't even look at him."

Mrs. Boggs stood silently for a minute, like there was

something she was trying to figure out whether or not she should say. "How do you think he gets all those bruises, May?"

I shrugged. "I don't know. Fighting with those wild brothers of his, probably."

"No." Mrs. Boggs shook her head. "That's not how."

"But then, how . . . ," I said. "Oh."

Oh.

And that's when I thought I understood what she was trying to tell me. "His daddy?"

Mrs. Boggs shook her head again. "No. His stepmother. I think she takes it out on him instead of his half brothers, because he's the oldest, and he's not hers."

Stepmother? Half brothers? Now, that surprised me. "None of them are his full brothers? Not even Jackson?"

"No."

I tried putting myself in his shoes. I supposed it would be tough to live in such a small home with a family you were made to feel only half a part of. "Has he talked to you about it?"

"Not exactly," Mrs. Boggs said, rubbing her forehead in a tired sort of way. "He said something to me once that hinted at what was going on, and I've talked to the guidance counselor, the principal. I've reported it. But he won't admit what's happening in the words he needs to make it real. But maybe if he comes with us, he will. At the very least, we can give him a break. Please, May. I know it's hard, and it sounds like his friends haven't done right by you, but try to open your heart toward him. He needs it."

I don't know if this made me a bad person, because while I felt sorry for Tommy's situation, I still didn't want him to tag along. But I also had the feeling that if I said no, Mrs. Boggs would bring him along anyway.

I sighed. "Fine. I guess he can come."

"Good girl," Mrs. Boggs said. "And you'll talk to him? You won't ice him out?"

I sighed once more, for good measure. "No, ma'am."

Mrs. Boggs patted me on the back. "Thank you."

Once Mrs. Boggs had gotten her cell phone out of the RV, her and Tommy went outside to call Tommy's father.

When they came back a few minutes later, Tommy was grinning from ear to ear. "I'm coming," Tommy announced. "My first road trip!"

I tried not to let myself look disappointed. "Oh . . . that's great."

Behind Tommy, Mrs. Boggs nodded at me.

Tommy threw himself down on the couch and patted his stomach. "You got any food around here? I'm starving."

Instead of feeling annoyed with him, I tried again to put myself in Tommy's shoes. Momma would *never* hurt me. Ever. It must have been hard to go home to a place where he didn't even feel safe. So like Mrs. Boggs said, I opened up my heart.

"You can have one of my Tootsie Pops. They're up front. You can take any flavor you want."

Then I realized maybe opening my heart a tiny bit was enough. So I added, "But don't you dare touch any of the orange ones. I'm saving those for my momma."

. * . + * .

Before Mrs. Boggs finally went to take her afternoon rest, she put her hands on her hips and looked around. "This place is a mess."

She was right. It *was* a mess. Books lay splayed open here and there, and things had rattled off the shelves and out of cardboard boxes onto the floor.

"Yeah," agreed Tommy, looking around. "No kidding."

"Tommy," I said. "That's rude."

Mrs. Boggs ignored him. "If we're going on a week-long trip, we should try to get this place organized. And since I'll be doing all the driving, that particular task will fall on the two of you. No free rides from me, I'll tell you that much right now. So go on and get started. And I want each of you to pick a book to read, too."

"Aww," moaned Tommy.

"And here's a refresher, since you're new to the crew," she said, eyeing Tommy. "We wake up at nine. I'll do a few hours of driving. Lunch at noon, and then I like to take some time to rest and be alone. I expect you two to either read or organize while I'm in my room. No free rides, no idle minds. That's the deal. Choose whatever book looks most interesting, as long as it's not something you've read before. No cheating and no lying." She looked at us both with a warning in her eyes. "That's part of the deal also."

The last of her words rang in my ears. *No cheating and no lying.* I knew she was talking about the books, but still. I was already lying, since I hadn't told her the full truth of what this whole journey was actually about.

And with that, she disappeared into her bedroom and shut the door.

"I know she can seem it, but she's not actually *that* strict," Tommy said. "She's only strict if you act up. If you don't, she's actually one of the nicest teachers I've ever had. I think she might be my favorite teacher of all time. Even more than Mr. Beauregard, my first-grade teacher, who gave us each a little bag of candy every Friday afternoon."

"Okay. Fine. Then let's do a good job cleaning for her." And since I wasn't particularly in the mood to talk to Tommy, I added, "And let's be quiet so she can have a nice rest."

I thought I had an idea of how much stuff Mrs. Boggs had simply from the look of the place, but truly, I'd had no idea. All the boxes were stuffed so full, I worried their sides might split open any second. It was a miracle the Winnebago could even move an inch, weighed down as it was.

I started poking around in one of the boxes stacked behind the leather armchair up front. It was full of men's clothes. The box next to it was full of men's clothes, too.

"Mr. Boggs was an engineer, you know," Tommy said. He was sitting cross-legged next to an open box he had pulled out from beneath the dining table. A few science textbooks and engineering manuals were piled up in front of him, as well as a few pairs of worn-out men's shoes. "That's who all this stuff belongs to, I think. He helped build things for a living. Computer software. Isn't that cool? It's sad he's gone. Mrs. Boggs said he would have liked me. He passed on a few years ago."

"I already knew that," I said. Even if Mrs. Boggs hadn't been my teacher, I still knew some things about her, and about Mr. Boggs, too. "Last night, Mrs. Boggs brought me to see his gravestone in the cemetery so I could give him my regards. His first name was Darryl. He thought science was a certain kind of magic."

"Yeah. He was only forty-one when he died," Tommy added. "That's how old my dad is."

"That's not very old," I said quietly. All of a sudden I

wasn't in the mood to compete about who knew more about Mr. Boggs. "She must have been so sad."

Tommy glanced at the closed bedroom door. "I think she still is."

We fell back into silence after that. As I sorted through the books, I noticed that their pages made a whirring, buzzing kind of noise when I thumbed through them fast enough. I grabbed my recorder to capture the sound of it, my back to Tommy so he wouldn't bother me with questions about what I was doing. As I recorded it, I imagined that it wasn't a whirring I was hearing, but the author whispering the words to me really, really quickly.

We'd only been quiet for about ten minutes when Tommy piped up again.

"Hey, May?"

I was trying to consolidate the men's clothes—Mr. Boggs's, I assumed—into one box, but it was proving near impossible. I didn't look up at Tommy. "Yeah?"

"Where are we going, anyway?"

"Up to Nashville."

"Oh. That's cool."

"Yup."

Another few minutes of silence passed. "Hey, May?"

I stifled a sigh. "What?"

"*Why* are we going to Nashville?"

I swallowed hard. Somehow, the excitement of the

adventure had made me forget the reason it was all happening. "I'm signed up to sing in a contest."

Tommy was now throwing a book in the air so it spun in fast circles. "Oh, that's cool. I didn't know you liked to sing. I've heard your momma strumming her guitar, but I never hear you making any noise. Are you any good? What song are you going to sing?"

I tried swallowing again, but found that I couldn't. My mouth and my throat had gone completely dry. I squeezed my eyes shut and tried not to imagine the huge crowd, stretching out in front of me.

I tried not to think about how it would feel to be alone onstage, opening my mouth, only to have no sound come out at all.

Thinking about it was enough to make my hands shake. People would fidget. Then they would feel uncomfortable, watching me all frozen and scared up there on the stage. Maybe someone would even start to laugh.

My daddy would be watching, too. Eventually, he would have to look away. That's how embarrassed he'd feel for me. Embarrassed and . . .

Ashamed.

"May?" Tommy said. "You okay?"

Suddenly it felt like the air inside the RV had turned to stone and was about to crush in on me. "I'm going to be sick."

I got up from the floor and dashed into Mrs. Boggs's bathroom, slamming the door shut behind me.

Once I finished throwing up, I sat on the bathroom floor and rocked back and forth. I pretended Momma was in there, sitting with me. I didn't need to think about the singing part right now. Maybe the idea of what song to sing would come to me if I wasn't spending every second of the day worrying about it. I had a couple of days. I could at least *try* to enjoy myself. And the best way to do that was to pretend the final destination didn't include me standing on a stage with a microphone in my hand. No. I would think about all that later.

After a couple of minutes, I splashed some cold water on my face and went back to organizing in silence. And somehow this time, so did Tommy.

CHAPTER 12

Mrs. Boggs only wanted to drive for another hour once she came out of her bedroom, so we had to stop in Baton Rouge for the night, even though that hadn't been the plan.

We parked at the edge of a big Walmart parking lot, which was in a shopping center with a Texas Roadhouse, a Cracker Barrel, and a restaurant called Back Yard Burgers. Mrs. Boggs said Walmart stores all around the country let you park an RV overnight for free, if you minded your manners and only stayed the one night.

While Tommy begged Mrs. Boggs for burgers for dinner (she said, "No, absolutely not," and rattled on about saturated fats), I tried to get my bearings. How far were we from my old house? I wondered. I had paid close attention to each turn we took once we got off the interstate, but in all the years we lived in Baton Rouge, Momma and I had never been to this particular Walmart in this part of town. How far was Rosa's house from here? Would she be excited if she knew I was back in town, or would she not even care?

Mrs. Boggs made tuna fish sandwiches on healthy brown bread with a side of celery sticks for supper. She seemed distracted. She didn't even scold Tommy for mooning on and on about the Back Yard Burgers sign out the window. She barely touched her sandwich and only responded to questions with single-word answers. Her mind seemed miles away from her body.

I knew that feeling because it was happening to me at that exact moment, too. Being back in Baton Rouge was strange. Coming back was all I'd dreamt of since we moved to Davenport.

But to my surprise, being back wasn't the good kind of strange.

As we ate, I couldn't help but think about Gram and my old house, where I had my own room that was painted a pretty shade of purple. Lavender, Momma called it. We lived close to a little shopping center with an ice cream shop we walked to sometimes if Momma got back from work early enough.

Before I'd ruined everything.

The memory of that terrible day stayed with me

always, like one of those sharp, stubborn burs that digs itself into your sock and doesn't let go.

We were at Gram's house. I only went over when my grandfather was out and about. I loved it there because they had their own swimming pool, a big backyard with thick green grass, and a burbling fountain that attracted singsongy birds from all over the neighborhood. Gram and I were fixing to bake a pie, but she didn't have all the ingredients we needed. She let me go up and hang out in Momma's old room while she ran to the store.

I was in a happy mood that day. I was good-tired from spending the afternoon in the pool, and I knew I had a slice of Gram's pecan pie in my future. So as I lay on Momma's old bed, I closed my eyes and started to sing. Even though I was too old for lullabies, I still liked to sing Momma's song whenever I was alone. I didn't even need to think about the lyrics because Momma had sung them to me so many times, it was like they were written on my heart. The house was empty, so I really let myself get carried away with it.

I was only halfway through when the door to Momma's room opened.

It was my grandfather.

"Maybelle. What are you doing here?"

The expression on his face was like he had come home to find a stranger in his house. I suppose we *were* strangers, in a way, because we almost never spent time together, not like Gram and I did. He signed my birthday cards, but that was about it. And he didn't speak to Momma *at all*.

Sometimes I felt like I wasn't his granddaughter so much as a reminder of the "sin" Momma committed by having me out of wedlock.

Look harder, I wanted to beg him. Because if he only looked harder, he'd see that I was so much more.

But, of course, that's not what I said.

"Uh, I was with Gram. We were going to bake a pie. A pecan pie. Sir."

"Is that so?"

I nodded. He kept on staring at me. The silence was starting to whine terribly, so I started talking to drown it out. "Um, yes. And I'd also like to thank you, sir. For your generosity. Momma and I love our house, and I know we wouldn't be able to live there if it wasn't for your help with the rent. So thank you. Sir."

When I finished, his eyeballs nearly popped right out of his skull. "What? Help with your rent? What are you talking about?"

As soon as he said it, I understood. It was a secret. *He* wasn't the one helping us with money—Gram was. And he had no idea.

I still remember the way Momma cried and cried the day we had to pack everything up.

"I'm so sorry I can't help you anymore," Gram said to Momma when she came to say goodbye. She was crying, too, but unlike Momma, Gram was trying to hide it. She kept pressing the palm of her hand to the corner of her eyes, like she didn't want to mess up her makeup. "You know how your father can get, Gemma. Stubborn as a mule."

While they talked, I was sick with worry Gram would tell Momma it had been all my fault that he found out, but she never did. I carried that knowledge inside me like it was a poison all my own, eating me up from the inside.

We went to look at a few apartments in Baton Rouge, but I could tell Momma's heart wasn't in it. She kept saying it might be good for us to have a fresh start.

I desperately didn't want to leave Baton Rouge, but I didn't let myself cry or complain about it. I didn't deserve to be sad. Momma thanked me again and again for how strong I was being, which only made me feel worse. I played that day at Gram's house over and over in my head, and I kept coming back to one thing.

If only I hadn't been singing, none of this would have happened.

If only I had made no noise at all.

About a week after we lost our home, Momma lost her job. It wasn't even that she did anything wrong—her boss at Magnolia Guitars was retiring and wanted to close the place down. Momma joked that it was the icing on the worst cake she'd ever eaten. For a few weeks we bounced around, staying with friends and then friends of friends. Sometimes I felt like we were wearing out our welcome before we even rang the doorbell to say hello.

And that's when Momma's friend Cynthia helped us out. She got Momma a job in Davenport *and* got us a spot to live at in Pelican Park. Cynthia's cousin was the manager, and even though he said he already had a waiting list, Cynthia sweet-talked him into bumping us to the top of it. And then she also put down the cash deposit for us because Momma didn't have the money right then.

I'd never liked Cynthia much (and especially not her boyfriends), but what she did for us was a real decent thing to do: she helped us at a time when we needed it the most. People can be confusing like that.

And then finally, a couple of weeks later, I couldn't handle it anymore. I told Momma the truth.

"Thank you for being so amazing through all this," she was saying. It felt like the hundredth time she'd praised me like this. Praise I most certainly did not deserve. So I broke.

"Stop telling me how good I am! I'm not good. This whole thing is my fault."

"What? What do you mean?"

And so I came clean. I told her everything.

"I'm so sorry," I said again and again.

She shushed me and hugged me for a long, long time.

She told me it wasn't my fault. She'd never told me it was a secret I was supposed to keep, she said, and that was her fault, and not mine. But I couldn't shake the feeling. Like a piece of gum that had gotten stuck in my hair, the guilt stayed put.

Even with Momma's forgiveness, I couldn't forgive myself.

* * * * *

It was time for bed before I knew it. Mrs. Boggs made up the couch for me, as usual, and put down an extra blanket to soften the floor beneath Tommy's sleeping bag.

I changed into my favorite astronaut-cat pajamas and brushed my teeth in the bathroom. When I was done, I spotted a bit of toothpaste foam at the corner of my mouth. I wiped it off. I touched my lips. I had a near-identical copy of Momma's mouth, even though my smiles were nowhere near as nice as hers because I didn't have her dimples. My nose was also like hers, small and round, but my eyes—mine were much lighter and greener than Momma's light brown, and they had a touch of gold near the center. Were those my daddy's eyes looking back at me?

When I came out, Tommy looked over at me and grinned.

I scowled at him. "What are you looking at?"

Tommy grinned even wider. "I like your pajamas."

I looked down. Momma and I had found them half-off and nearly split our sides laughing about the terrified expression on the astronaut cat's face, like it had been launched into outer space without its permission.

I loved those pajamas. But somehow they seemed way less funny and way more stupid when Tommy O'Brien was looking at them. I scowled harder. "Mind your own business, won't you?"

After Mrs. Boggs said good night and flicked off the lights, Tommy fell asleep in ten seconds flat.

Me? I was wide awake. I lay there for what felt like hours and hours, tossing and turning beneath the scratchy wool blanket. Finally, I got up and off the couch, grabbed my recorder from my bag, and slipped outside.

The Walmart parking lot was empty, except for a few deserted cars. Even though it was late, the pavement still glowed with the heat of the day. If only my pocket radio was still working. I didn't have the nerve to ask Mrs. Boggs to turn on WKBC for my daddy's show. My daddy and I didn't share a name or anything like that, but Mrs. Boggs was sharp. I feared she would sniff out the truth about the whole thing, so I went without.

Other than the buzz and flicker of the streetlamps and the occasional whiz of a car passing by on the I-10, the parking lot was also empty of sound. There was nothing for me to record.

In fact, it was so quiet, the only thing I could hear was the rattle of my thoughts and the thump of my heart.

I was out of sorts being back in Baton Rouge, no doubt about it. But I don't think that's what was keeping me awake.

It was the contest. I was so nervous, just the idea of picking out a song had made me sick. And I wasn't even on the stage yet. What if I couldn't find the courage to face my stage fright? If I was going to wow my daddy, I had to. I had to find a way.

But what if I couldn't?

You can't, said my head.

You can, thumped my heart.

CHAPTER 13

Mrs. Boggs didn't want to get out of bed the next morning. She said through her door she had a headache and needed to rest. I knocked, and offered to bring her some water or maybe some Tylenol, but she said she wanted to be left alone.

"Should we call a doctor?" I asked Tommy.

"Nah." His blond hair was sticking up every which way from a night of sleeping on the floor. "Jaycee—that's my stepmom—sometimes she gets headaches like that. Bedaches, I call them. Because when she gets one, she doesn't get out of bed for the whole day."

He must have seen the alarm on my face, because he shook his head and said, "Don't worry. They go away on their own. Anyways, Mrs. Boggs is already showing herself to be better about handling one than Jaycee. *Much* better. Jaycee only gets them after she gets into a really bad mood, lots of screaming and hollering and—" Almost like he couldn't stop himself, Tommy's fingers went to his bruised eye.

I thought of Mrs. Boggs's quest to get Tommy to talk to her about what was going on at his home. So I inched forward. "And what?"

Tommy's hands fell back down to his sides. "Never mind."

It was a hard and heavy kind of "never mind," a "never mind" that told me to stop asking questions because they'd yield me no answers. So I shrugged and turned to one of the boxes I had only half finished going through the day before. "I'm going to clean and organize some more while she rests."

Tommy reached out and touched my shoulder. "Wait— May?"

"Yeah?"

"I wanted to say . . . I wanted you to know . . . I'm sorry. About the way Jeremiah treats you. He can be all kinds of ugly."

I fixed Tommy with a stare. His cheeks were growing pinker and pinker by the second. "Then why are you friends with him?"

He fiddled with the edges of a book. "I don't know. Because everyone thinks that's where I belong, I guess. With the other bad kids."

Something inside me softened toward Tommy right

then. Because in only a day, I'd already seen glimpses that made me think maybe Mrs. Boggs was right. That Tommy wasn't one of the bad kids after all. "Thank you. For saying sorry."

We spent the rest of the morning cleaning and organizing while Mrs. Boggs slept. I figured it would be best to put away some of her books up in the kitchen cabinets so they wouldn't rattle and shake onto the floor when she started driving again. *If* she started driving again.

I wasn't going to shove her books any which way, willy-nilly. I had to organize them first. There were all sorts of novels—some meant for kids and others for adults—and just as many books of poetry, some by authors I'd learned about in school and others I hadn't. Many of the books were filled with notes in a spindly script I suspected belonged to Mrs. Boggs, and their covers were faded and their spines creased.

Well loved. That's what Momma would have called them.

Part of me wished I'd been put in remedial language arts this past year. I would've liked to learn about books from a woman who loved them that hard.

While sorting through the piles, I found a book of my own to read during our journey. I chose *The Wonderful Wizard of Oz,* because my middle name was Dorothy, like the main character in the story. I had seen the movie, but I didn't realize it was a book, too.

Tommy wasn't much help at all. After less than an hour, he took a family-size packet of string cheese from the fridge and sat in the leather recliner with *Introduction to Mechanical Engineering* open on his lap.

"Aren't you even going to pretend to help me organize?" I asked.

"My blood sugar is low," he said, already ripping into his third string cheese. "Plus, I'm reading. I'm organizing my brain."

"Yeah, right," I said. No way, no how, was he actually reading a textbook that dense and boring-looking.

It didn't take long for Tommy to fall dead asleep with his mouth open, cheese stick wrappers all down the front of his dirty T-shirt.

"Boys," I grumbled to myself.

I kept on organizing, though. I figured if I did a good enough job, it might help ease the pain of Mrs. Boggs's headache.

When I went to put the books away in the cabinets above the stove, my fingers brushed what felt like soft, buttery leather. Whatever it was didn't feel like a normal kitchen supply. I couldn't see what it was from where I stood, so I grabbed a pair of cooking tongs from the drawer and used them to pull it down.

It was a photo album. I wiped the cover clean of dust and tipped it open.

The album was filled with pictures of a round, happy-looking young woman and a tall, handsome man with dark brown skin and a bald head. In the pictures, he was usually stooping over or bending down to wrap his arms around her. In some of the pictures, he was kissing her on the cheek, and in others, both their heads were thrown back in laughter.

Wait a second— I squinted my eyes and looked closer.

The woman was Mrs. Boggs.

She had on the most beautiful, colorful clothes, and they didn't seem at all like the kind of clothes she wore now—the Mrs. Boggs I knew wore crisp gray shirts and black slacks. But *these* clothes were all the shades of the rainbow and then some. Fuchsia silk dresses, emerald-green pants, sunflower-yellow blouses. Lavender head-scarves and orange skirts. But it wasn't just her clothes that were different. In the pictures, her smile lit up her whole face. She smiled like the world was so beautiful, she might cry from the joy of it. I was flipping through, page by page, when—

"I haven't seen that album in years. I forgot it was even up there."

Mrs. Boggs was standing right there behind me. She must have come out of her bedroom without me notic-ing. I jumped back, feeling like I'd been caught rifling through a drawer full of her undergarments.

"I—I'm sorry, I was trying to get the books put away, and this was up there, blocking the shelf. I shouldn't have snooped."

She didn't say anything. She came over to see the page I was looking at. "We were so young. Wasn't Darryl handsome?"

I nodded. "You both look so happy."

She flipped to the next page. In this one, an even younger Mrs. Boggs was wearing a graduation robe and tasseled hat, standing between a man with a big smile and a woman with her same curly brown hair. I've never seen two people look more proud in all my life.

"My parents," she said, touching their faces. "This was right after Darryl and I graduated from UC Berkeley. My parents loved that I went there, because I was so close to home."

On the other page was a picture of her and Darryl, throwing their tasseled hats into the air with huge smiles on their faces.

"Our future felt like a promise back then." Mrs. Boggs stared at the photograph and sighed. "A lot can change in twenty years."

I traced my finger along the pink dress Mrs. Boggs was wearing in one of the photographs. "Why'd you stop wearing all these beautiful clothes?"

She stared at the photo for a long minute. "When

Darryl died, it felt like all the color drained out of the world. I suppose the color drained right out of me, too."

She tipped the album shut and pushed it away. "My headache's gone, so I've got a few hours of driving in me. I figure we can reach Mississippi by nightfall. And, May?"

"Yes, ma'am?"

She looked at the album. "Please put that away. I don't want to see it again."

I did as I was told, though I wanted to keep looking. I found it strange that she would get rid of her own beautiful things but, at the same time, hold on to all of Mr. Boggs's most boring possessions, like old engineering manuals and his worn-out football slippers.

The reasons why people do the things they do can be as unknowable as the universe of stars swirling above our heads.

CHAPTER 14

Late in the afternoon, about an hour and a half past the outskirts of Baton Rouge, we passed the Louisiana state line. I put down my book and held my breath as we crossed. It was my first time out of Louisiana, but the same as on my birthday every year, nothing felt new or different about me, even though I hoped it would.

Right by the state line was a sign that said WELCOME TO MISSISSIPPI: BIRTHPLACE OF AMERICA'S MUSIC. I watched it grow closer and then disappear. I'm pretty sure that sign was talking about the blues. I knew from Momma that the blues music she so loved had grown up in the Mississippi Delta.

Momma had first talked to me about the blues after I had gone to see her perform at the Pit Stop. It was the first time her boss let her choose her own music instead of covers of popular country songs. She sang a couple of songs she'd written herself in her own funky sort of style, which had tiny whispers of the blues, but that was it. She sang some country and did an acoustic cover of a pop song or two. But she didn't do a single blues song. Frankly, I was surprised. Momma loved the blues, so why wasn't she playing them? On the way home, I asked her why not.

"Because I wouldn't feel quite right about it. I respect the blues. I adore the blues with every inch of my music-loving heart. But they'll never be *mine*, exactly. Does that make sense?"

I shook my head.

"Music is a story, May. And if I played the blues, it would always feel like a cheap imitation of the real thing, because it isn't my story to tell. Which is why I like to try to do my own thing. Chords and melodies that are a little funky and folksy and that tell the story of me, Gemma Lane—that's the best kind of music there is. You know why? Because it's true. And it comes from here." She tapped her chest. "It doesn't come from something you took from someone else."

I never fully understood what she meant by that, but just thinking about the blues and that conversation made my heart ache for Momma. Leaving Louisiana felt like a string connecting me to her had been snipped. We had spoken briefly on the phone the day before, but her service was no good—her voice kept cutting in and out. Apparently, there was some unexpected rough and stormy weather in the Bahamas. She said she was fine and not to worry about her, but of course, I worried anyway. And it only made me miss her even worse.

"I want to get off the interstate," Mrs. Boggs said. "I'm sick of all the strip malls and flashing signs. I need some natural beauty."

She told us we were going to take the "scenic route" up to Jackson, on a road called the Natchez Trace Parkway.

"Will it take us much longer?" I asked anxiously.

"Don't worry. We've got time."

We stopped for gas before changing over from the interstate to the parkway. Mrs. Boggs went into the store to pay and came back out with a paper receipt and three little cards. She handed one to Tommy and then one to me.

At the top it said:

$$ GOLD RUSH TRIPLER $$
WIN UP TO $1,000!

It had a line that said WINNING NUMBERS, with four circles with question marks inside them, and below that there were a bunch of glittery gold dollar signs.

Mrs. Boggs gave both me and Tommy a penny. "It's

a scratch-off. Match any of those dollar signs with the numbers up here, and you win. Got it?"

"Yes, ma'am," I said.

"Why'd you get these?" Tommy asked.

Mrs. Boggs slid into the front seat of the RV and rifled through the cup holder, looking for a penny for herself. "It's a tradition. Darryl and I always bought scratch-off lottery tickets whenever we went on a road trip."

"Did you ever win?" Tommy asked.

"Of course not," Mrs. Boggs said, tutting her tongue. "Don't be silly. No one ever wins at these things. That was never the point."

"Then what *was* the point?"

"Fun," Mrs. Boggs said. "Fun was the point."

We all fell silent as we rubbed away the little gold dollar signs, the soft *scritchy-scritchy-scritchy* of our coins against the golden tickets the only sound filling the RV.

"Nope," Tommy said. "I got nothing."

"A dud for me as well," Mrs. Boggs said with a sigh. "May?"

"One sec." I was going slow. As I scratched, the ink fell away like eraser dust. I blew it off to see if I had won anything.

I stared at it. I had three squares that said JACKPOT! And next to them were small gold dollar signs. "I think . . . I think I got something," I breathed.

But it couldn't be. I never won anything.

"May I?" Mrs. Boggs motioned at my card.

I held my breath as I gave it to her.

She looked at my card for only a second before she started to laugh.

"What?" Tommy said. "What is it?"

Mrs. Boggs wiped at her eyes. "The universe is funny, that's all. Congratulations, May. You've got a winning ticket."

"What?" I leapt up from my seat, my heart knocking against my chest. "I did? How much?"

"The grand prize." Mrs. Boggs started laughing again. "One thousand dollars."

"It can't be," I said, refusing to believe it. "I've got terrible luck."

Both Momma and I did. We weren't the kind of people who won things or got good news. We were the other sort of people. The sort of people that got news about flat tires and overdue rent checks.

Mrs. Boggs smiled at me. "Well then, young lady, it looks like your luck is changing."

"Mrs. Boggs is right!" Tommy said, after scrambling to look over her shoulder. "You won, May! One *thousand* dollars! You're rich!"

Tommy dropped to his knees and howled like a wolf, which made Mrs. Boggs laugh even more. Soon enough, even *I* was laughing and clapping my hands together. It was true—I really had won!

Once we had all settled down, Mrs. Boggs hurried back into the gas station, holding my winning ticket to her chest. Part of me still thought there had to be some mistake, but when she came back out a few minutes later, she didn't have the ticket. She had a pile of cash.

Mrs. Boggs handed the stack of bills to me when she got back inside. I had never seen so much money in my whole life.

And it was all mine.

"Can I touch it?" Tommy whispered.

"Sure," I said, handing it over to him.

"Wow," he said. "Imagine all the cool stuff you'll be able to buy with this. Congratulations, May." He handed the pile back to me with a big smile on his face. "This is the coolest thing ever."

He was happy for me. Honestly, truly happy I'd won. I could see it in his eyes. But . . . I hadn't done anything special to win. Mrs. Boggs had bought the tickets and passed them out to us randomly—it was the luck of the draw that had put the winning ticket into my hands, and not in Tommy's. It didn't feel right that I got to keep it all and Mrs. Boggs and Tommy got none.

And so I did the only thing that felt right. I counted out the stack of my winnings into three equal piles. When I was finished, I handed one pile to Mrs. Boggs and then one to Tommy.

"Here," I said to the both of them. "I split it up as best I could. More than three hundred dollars for each of us."

Tommy stared at the money I'd given him like he was afraid it would poof into dust if he blinked. "You don't mean . . . is this for *me*?"

"Yep," I said, smiling at him.

Tommy howled again. "*Aaahhh-ooooh!* Thank you, May! Thank you!"

"You're welcome." I felt like blushing from my toes to my ears. Who knew that giving part of it away would feel a million times better than winning it in the first place?

"Oh, May," Mrs. Boggs said, trying to push the money back at me. "No. I couldn't possibly. You're the lucky winner. You should keep it. Split it between the two of you."

"No," I said, shaking my head. "Keep it. Please. We're all in this together."

Mrs. Boggs squeezed my hand quickly before she tucked the money into the cup holder. "I suppose we are."

Right away, I peeled one hundred dollars of my winnings and stuffed it deep into my backpack and zipped it up tight. A pressure on my heart eased. I could pay Momma back for the lost emergency money after all.

Once Mrs. Boggs started up the RV and got back on the road, Tommy could barely sit still. He counted and recounted his bills—out loud, then silently, then out loud again. Then he started running the length of the RV, back and forth, jumping over boxes, yelling about the things he was going to buy.

"A new bike with blinking lights! No, an Xbox! And three pounds of candy corn! Or a robot! One of those robot vacuum cleaners! A hamster! A hamster cage! No, one of those hamster palaces! With the wheels and the colored tubes! Or a lightsaber! A set of lightsabers! A Darth Vader costume! Or—"

"You've created a monster," Mrs. Boggs said, smiling a little at the long, country road unspooling in front of us.

I nodded. "No kidding."

We had switched over to the Natchez Trace Parkway by then. Even if it was going to take us longer to get up north, I could hardly be mad about it, because it was so beautiful. There were peaceful swamps and babbling streams and miles and miles of eyeball-popping green. Green trees, green bushes, long, lush green grass. No garbage on the road, no blinking signs for casinos or bars.

Eventually, Tommy tired himself out and lay down on the floor, using his money as a pillow. He was asleep in less than a minute. The silence was a welcome reprieve.

Mrs. Boggs looked over at me. I was riding up front with her, in my copilot seat. "What will you do with your winnings, May? You've certainly been quiet."

For the last fifteen miles or so, I was quiet because I'd been thinking. Specifically, I'd been thinking about the Cowardly Lion from *The Wonderful Wizard of Oz*. I thought about how he had been fearful his whole life, but the great wizard changed all that by giving him a dish of courage to drink.

If only courage was a thing someone could give to you. Something you could buy. *That's* what I would spend my money on.

But all I said was, "I don't know yet. What about you?"

"Oh, I know *exactly* what I'm going to do with it."

"What?" I asked, scooching forward in my chair. "What is it?"

"You'll see. It's a surprise."

CHAPTER 15

That night we parked the RV at a campground off the Natchez Trace Parkway. It was nothing like camping out in a Walmart parking lot. It was like camping in the middle of the wildest patch of wilderness. Once evening descended, the bugs were so loud, I could barely even hear myself think. And the mosquitoes. So many mosquitoes! I wanted to stay inside in the blissful air-conditioning, but Mrs. Boggs didn't let me. She said I had to get a healthy dose of forest air into my lungs.

Even though it was still so hot that my tank top was sticking to my stomach, Mrs. Boggs bought a bundle of firewood and made us a campfire. "The smoke keeps the bugs away. You'll see."

She was right. Soon the air around our campsite was thick and smoky, and all the mosquitoes vanished. The three of us sat there by the fire after dinner, beneath the stars. Tommy kept throwing stuff into the flames, and Mrs. Boggs had to tell him to stop ten different times. But I wasn't watching the fire; I was watching the stars. I had no idea they could ever look like that, like thousands of lightning bugs shining and glittering in a sea of black. I stared at the sky for so long, my neck got a crick in it.

"Oh no," Mrs. Boggs said, once we'd all gone inside. She had already gotten ready for bed. "I forgot to put the last of the fire out. Have you seen where I put my shoes?"

"I'll do it," I offered.

After Mrs. Boggs explained to me where the water-spout was on the edge of our site and how to stay away from the steam, I went back outside. As I waited for the bucket to fill up, the stars winked at me, like they knew I was watching. Even though there weren't any shooting stars, I still made a wish. The campfire had turned into a bunch of ruby-colored embers by then, smoldering and smoking and crackling and popping. Before I poured water on it, I recorded the sounds of the dying fire and tried not to think about how much I missed Momma.

The next morning, Mrs. Boggs made us scrambled eggs, and she spent all of breakfast teasing us about the big surprise she had coming up later that day.

When we left the campsite, I sat up front with her at first. The view out the front was pretty much the same as the day before. The Natchez Trace Parkway was only a two-lane road, so cars kept piling up behind Mrs. Boggs, who was driving even slower than usual because she wanted a chance to look at all the pretty scenery, too. Trucks and cars zoomed dangerously around us, laying on their horns.

"Okay, sweetheart," said Mrs. Boggs calmly, to a man careening by in a red pickup truck. "No problem, go right ahead. After you."

I giggled. Mrs. Boggs had a funny way of saying real polite things under her breath to other drivers, but beneath the nice words, it felt like she was actually cussing them out.

After a while, I got bored, so I went back to see what Tommy was doing.

He had one of the engineering textbooks open on one side of him, and in front of him, he had a digital alarm clock all taken apart. All of its wires and little metal plates and pieces were exposed, reminding me of my broken vintage Gran Prix.

"What are you doing?"

"The clock's broken," he said. He grinned when I raised my eyebrow. "I mean, it was broken before I took it apart. I'm trying to fix it for Mrs. Boggs."

I leaned forward. "Can you show me what you're doing?"

Tommy looked up at me, surprised. "You really want to know?"

"Yeah. Sure."

A goofy grin spread across his face. "All right. Yeah. Cool."

He pointed at a skinny piece of green metal. "See this? This is the circuit board. This is like the electronic brain of the clock. It's the most important piece, kind of like the brains in our own heads. . . ."

He went on and on. I didn't catch half of what Tommy said about this or that, but he grew more excited with every word. He was still explaining the importance of the teeniest, tiniest screw when Mrs. Boggs called out, "Hey, you two! We're almost there—to my surprise!"

Tommy and I levitated from our seats and ran to the windows.

We had gotten off the parkway by then, and the scenery had changed, too. All around us was a sea of flowers. Purple, pink, yellow, white—every color and shape imaginable. Flowers in bushes, on trees, planted in the ground, climbing up stony walls. Paths crisscrossed through the garden, people walking here and there.

When we drove a little farther, we came upon the most picturesque pond I'd ever seen, with white ducks and a huge fountain blasting out of its middle.

"Where *are* we, Mrs. Boggs?" Tommy asked.

"Take another look."

Then she turned another corner, and in front of us

was a huge building. There was a long, shady porch with people sitting on it, drinking iced tea and fanning themselves from the heat. Above them were at least ten flags— one was an American flag, and one of them was just a rainbow. A fancy sign above the entrance said MAGNOLIA'S RESORT AND SPA.

It was the nicest place I'd ever seen in my life. The hotel's white paint looked so fresh and clean, I imagined it could almost still be wet. Even more flowers were planted all along the pathway leading from the driveway to the porch.

Mrs. Boggs shut off the RV's engine. "Get your bags, you two. And, Tommy, fix your hair."

I looked at Tommy. He grinned and grabbed his duffel bag.

Once I had gathered my belongings, I joined Tommy and Mrs. Boggs outside. A young man in a polo shirt and pressed khaki pants took the RV keys from Mrs. Boggs and directed us inside.

A whoosh of chilled air met us as we went through the front door. A crystal chandelier hung from the ceiling, and there was a polished wooden desk at the back of the room with two huge glass vases filled to brimming with white flowers. There was also a small sign with golden lettering that said ALL ARE WELCOME HERE.

I smoothed my tank top down, suddenly aware of how wrinkled it was and how droopy its straps were. The sign might have said all were welcome, but I still felt like a lump of coal tossed into a bucket of diamonds. It was clear I didn't belong in a place like this.

But it seemed the woman behind the desk didn't notice, because she smiled at Mrs. Boggs and then at Tommy and me. "Hello, and welcome to Magnolia's."

"Alice Boggs, checking in," Mrs. Boggs said, leaning over the counter. "One standard room with two queen beds and a rollaway."

"Of course. Let me just find your reservation," she said as she started *clicker-clack*ing away on her computer.

Mrs. Boggs turned to us and smiled. *"This* is my surprise. We're going to stay here, courtesy of May's generosity in sharing her winnings. My parents stayed here two years ago after visiting me in Davenport and said they were treated like royalty. They tried to get me to come up with them, but I wasn't in the mood back then. I've wanted to check it out ever since. I called to make a reservation when I went to buy the firewood last night. They've got an award-winning garden and two swimming pools—one inside, one outside. *And* room service."

I looked around. *We* were staying *here?* And they had a swimming pool! I loved to swim. Gram used to call me her little fish, because I could swim the length of her pool in one go without having to come up for a breath. I couldn't remember the last time I'd been swimming.

"That's amazing!" Tommy cried. "Thanks, Mrs. Boggs!"

131

Part of me expected things to go wrong—they wouldn't be able to find our reservation, the credit card would be declined, something like that—but nothing did. In fact, the opposite happened.

"Hmm," the woman behind the counter said, frowning at her screen. "That's odd. Seems we're all booked up on our standard rooms. But I *do* have a two-bedroom suite I can upgrade you to. Free of charge, of course, as an apology for the mix-up." And then she looked up and winked at me.

After that, the nice man in the khaki pants put our bags on a golden luggage rack and showed us to our suite. To get there, we had to walk down a long hallway that went on for ages, almost like a skinny, carpeted runway.

Tommy and I had to share one of the bedrooms, but each of us got our own bed. Tommy kicked off his shoes and immediately started jumping on his.

"Look, we've got a flat-screen TV! It's so big! And look, there's a mini-fridge underneath it! And look at that little glass jar of M&M's!"

I got onto my own bed and let myself sink back into the feather pillows. I ran my hand over the smooth sheets, which were whiter than an angel's wings. I was floating on a cloud made of silk. How was I ever going to get up?

Mrs. Boggs knocked on our door. She'd already changed into a white fluffy robe and matching white slippers and had a book tucked underneath her arm. "How do you two feel about a dip in the pool?"

Now *that* was the one thing that could get me up and out of that heavenly bed. But then I remembered.

"I didn't bring a bathing suit."

Secretly, I was glad. The one I had was a hand-me-down from Momma, and it was still way too big on me. Whenever I went swimming, it sagged around my middle like a wet plastic bag. If I felt stupid wearing my astronaut-cat pajamas in front of Tommy, I would have felt doubly stupid letting him see me in that baggy swimming suit.

"Well, it's a good thing you still have your lottery winnings, now, isn't it? Let me change, and we'll go into downtown Jackson."

"I don't even own a bathing suit," Tommy said, jumping down from his bed with a *thump*. "I'll go in my shorts. I'd rather spend my money on something else."

"Fine," Mrs. Boggs said. "But you're still coming with."

"Awww," Tommy moaned.

"Just give me ten minutes," Mrs. Boggs said. "And then we'll go."

"I'll meet you in the hallway!" I called out after her.

I grabbed my tape recorder and slipped out the door into the hallway. I'd noticed an ice machine a little way down that had made a funny *clunk-a-chunk-runk* sound when we passed by earlier. I sat down cross-legged in front of the machine and pressed the Record button. "Ice machine," I said evenly, "Magnolia's Resort and Spa."

I recorded the *clunk-a-chunk-runk* for about a minute before clicking the recorder off. When I did, I noticed a presence right behind me.

It was Tommy.

"How long have you been standing there?" I asked.

He shrugged. "A while. How come you do that? Record things, I mean. Different sounds. I've seen you doing it at school, and I noticed you doing it last night, by the campfire."

"I don't know," I said, shrugging. I hadn't told many people about my sound collecting. It felt strange to talk about. "I like doing it, I guess."

"But why the ice machine?" Tommy pressed. "What's interesting about that?"

Tommy asked in a way that made me feel like he wasn't asking because he thought it was stupid, but because he was actually curious. So instead of mumbling something and changing the subject, I told him the truth. "I like to find the sounds other people don't stop to notice. The quiet ones. Because they're interesting, too." I wiggled my tape recorder in the air. "And I want to make sure they're not forgotten."

"Dang. That's so cool."

"Thanks." I jumped to my feet and shoved my recorder

in my back pocket. The long, perfect hallway was suddenly calling to me. My feet itched; I could already feel the wind in my hair. "Want to race?"

Tommy took a step back and grinned at me in surprise. "Really? You want to?"

"Yeah," I said. "Starting now!"

I took off without a backward glance. For a few perfect moments, time stopped. I don't think I'd ever run so fast or felt so free.

But then a hotel room door opened, and a man in a bright red polo shirt stepped out. I didn't have time to slow down before I crashed straight into him.

"Oof!" The man stumbled back and banged into the wall.

I myself had been knocked to the floor. Tommy was next to me by then, helping me to my feet. "You okay, May?"

"I'm fine." I turned to the man and opened my mouth to apologize when—

"Watch where you're going! How dare you!" he said, shoving a finger in my direction. Only then did I realize his face had grown almost as red as his shirt. "Did you sneak in here? Look at the state of you."

I felt like I had been shrunk down. I was the size of a pebble, with that man looming over me. I knew I didn't belong in a place like this, and I'd gone and proved it.

"How dare *she*?" came a voice from behind me. It was

Mrs. Boggs, striding toward us with a look on her face like she was going into battle. "I think the question is, how dare *you*? How dare you talk to her that way?"

I nearly gasped. Mrs. Boggs was still calm and collected, peaceful like those still ponds we passed on the Natchez Parkway that looked like glassy mirrors. "Unruffled," Momma would say.

And yet her words seemed to crackle and pulse in the air around us, like thunder and lightning. I'm surprised the light fixtures on the ceiling didn't shake and rattle, that's how powerful they were. The man seemed to shrink to half his size, like a deflating puffer fish.

In that moment, I realized Momma wasn't the only one who knew how to use word magic. Mrs. Boggs did, too. And where Momma's magic was a plea, Mrs. Boggs's was a command.

Mrs. Boggs came and put her hands protectively on my shoulders. "This child has as much right to be here as you do. She obviously bumped into you by mistake. And she's a child. You're the adult."

"And *you're* the nanny!" the man countered. "You should have control of your wards!"

Mrs. Boggs stared at him. Hard. "I'm the nanny? Really? Huh. What about me says 'nanny' to you?"

The moment stretched out, long and thick.

The man's face grew redder. He looked from Mrs. Boggs to Tommy and me. "Because . . . you . . . they . . ."

"Let's see," Mrs. Boggs said. "It can't be my master's degree in education, because you wouldn't be able to see that. Hmm . . . let me think. What else could it possibly be?"

"I . . . I just thought . . ."

"I am not their nanny. Try to remember that the next time you make an assumption. Now apologize for speaking to Maybelle here in such a way."

The man swallowed. His face was now so red, it was almost purple. He turned to me. "I—I . . . I'm sorry."

I gaped. This was the second time she'd wrangled an apology for me from an unlikely sort.

She squeezed my shoulder. "Your turn."

"I'm sorry for bumping into you, sir. It was an accident."

He glanced from me to Mrs. Boggs. "I . . . that's okay."

"Good." Mrs. Boggs straightened her shoulders in a teacherly sort of way. "It's settled." Then she turned away from the man like he wasn't even there. "Tommy, May, let's go. I've called us a taxi so we don't have to navigate through downtown Jackson in the RV. It should be here any minute."

I was quiet the whole walk to the lobby. When we got outside, Tommy immediately jumped onto one of the luggage racks and started riding around on it like it was a go-kart. Before Mrs. Boggs could tell him off, I turned to her and asked, "How did you learn to do that?"

"Do what?"

"Put power into your words like that. When you were talking to that man."

Mrs. Boggs considered my question. "People will try to tell you it's the words themselves that are powerful, but that's not always true. It's also about how you wield them. And no one in this world will give you that power, May, so you've got to find it for yourself. Whether you're giving a speech, singing, writing poetry, or reprimanding a hotel guest, if you believe what you're saying, and if what you're saying is right, your words will shine. That make any sense?"

I thought about it. It did make sense, but I still didn't think I could ever make my words so powerful. Maybe one day, but not now. Not like that. "I think so. Thank you."

Then she chuckled. "I've also been a fifth-grade teacher for fifteen years. If you're going to control twenty wriggly eleven-year-olds, you better know how to command a room."

CHAPTER 16

The department store we went to in Jackson was bigger than any I'd ever been to. The first floor was three times as big as our cafeteria at school, with carpeted aisles and stacks of neatly folded clothes on polished wooden tables.

I found a bathing suit I liked almost immediately. It was bright purple with silver zigzags on it. I could imagine a figure skater or a gymnast wearing something like it on television.

I was making my way to the dressing room when I stopped. Looking around that store, filled with acres of beautiful clothes, got me thinking. I had brought a few different outfits as options for the contest, but everything I owned was worn-out or stained or frayed around the edges when I looked at it in the hard light of day. And now here I was, with a stack of scratch-off lottery dollars burning a hole in my pocket.

The girls' section had some of the most beautiful dresses I'd ever seen. I browsed around, touching this and that. How could I ever pick one?

And that's when I saw it: the dress of my dreams.

The top was shimmery and metallic, and it looked more like liquid silver than fabric. A silver sash separated the top from the skirt, which whispered like wings when I took it off the rack. The skirt was multilayered, and the underskirt had sequins and crystals sewn on it that sparkled through the top gauzy layers like stars.

I grabbed a simple white dress, too, with a single flower pinned at the shoulder. It wasn't nearly as pretty as the silver one, but Momma taught me that it was always a good idea to have a backup plan.

Mrs. Boggs sat in a purple velvet chair by the triple mirrors while I tried on the two dresses and the bathing suit. Tommy was off doing Lord knows what in the boys' department. Probably causing all sorts of trouble.

First I tried on the bathing suit, which was a mighty fine upgrade from the old one of Momma's. I didn't need to show it to Mrs. Boggs to know it was right.

I tried on the simple white dress next. I modeled it for Mrs. Boggs, who nodded her approval. "Very nice."

The dress didn't look quite right with my dirty sneakers, but it *was* pretty.

I went back into the dressing room, took the white dress off, and carefully, very carefully, pulled the silver one over my head. The lining was silky smooth. Nothing tugged or pulled, and it wasn't too roomy anywhere. It felt exactly right.

I turned to look at myself in the mirror. I gasped when I saw my reflection.

It was like I was wearing pure starlight.

The silver top glittered. The sequins shimmered and sparkled.

No. *I* shimmered and sparkled.

This, I thought. I could stand on a stage in this dress. I could sing a song in this dress. I twirled in it. I curtsied in it. I grinned and covered my mouth with my hands.

Then I caught a look at its price tag and my eyeballs nearly rolled back up into my skull. It was three times as expensive as the white dress, and ten times more expensive than any item of clothing Momma had ever bought for me. I had enough lottery money to buy it if I wanted, but it was close.

"May, come on out. Let us see!"

I tiptoed out, hoping the spell wouldn't be broken by her reaction. "So?" I asked. "What do you think?"

"My word," breathed Mrs. Boggs.

Tommy was there now, too, sitting cross-legged on the floor with his chin in his hand, looking bored. His eyes widened when he saw me. "You . . . you look . . ." His mouth opened and closed.

Mrs. Boggs smiled. "I think what he means to say is that you're a vision, Maybelle."

Tommy's face turned bright red. "Uh, yeah. Whatever that means."

"It's expensive." I chewed on my bottom lip. "I don't know."

"That's what scratch-off money should be for," Mrs. Boggs said. "Something you want but don't necessarily need. I think that dress fits the bill perfectly, don't you?"

"I guess it does." I smiled at myself in the mirror, and the dress winked back at me. "I think I'm going to get it."

"You won't regret it. It's a special dress, May."

While I changed back into my humdrum, normal clothes, Mrs. Boggs knocked and told me they'd be waiting for me outside the store. Apparently, Tommy had made some kind of mess in the boys' department, so the manager found us and told him he was no longer welcome in the store.

I wanted to wear my new bathing suit right away, so I had the woman scan the tag and clip it off me right there at the register. She wrapped up my silver-starlight dress in a white box with pink tissue paper that crinkled and *shush*ed, and she tied the whole thing up with a glittering silver ribbon. Even the packaging was perfect.

Panic rushed through me as I passed the money over, much more money than I should have ever spent on a dress, but as soon as I took the box beneath my arm, I felt good again. Better than good. *Great.*

Maybe you could buy courage after all.

CHAPTER 17

The rest of that summer afternoon at Magnolia's was one of the best days of my life. The only thing that could have made it better was if Momma had been there to enjoy it with us.

One of the swimming pools was *inside* the building. I'd never seen a swimming pool inside before, but there it was, the wavy pattern of water reflecting on the ceiling in wiggly lines of light.

Mrs. Boggs settled on one of the pool chairs in a corner and immediately buried her nose in a book. I hadn't even taken my shorts off before Tommy cannonballed into the deep end, not even stopping to take off his T-shirt.

It echoed across the room with a whooshing *KERplunk-splash!* and pool water sprayed the walls and all over my legs.

"That was a bigger splash than I meant to do," Tommy said sheepishly, once he came up for air. And then he started to laugh. And the thing about Tommy's laugh is that it's more of a goofy giggle, and it sounds like happy, fizzing bubbles. And it's contagious. Even more contagious than yawning. Because even though what he said wasn't all that funny, Mrs. Boggs and I started cracking up, too.

Once we all calmed down, I took my recorder out of my shorts pocket. I almost didn't bring it, but I'd learned the hard way that whenever I didn't have it was when I found the best sounds to record. Like now. "Hey, Tommy—would you jump in again?"

Tommy happily obliged. I made him do cannonball after cannonball until I got the perfect recording of the splash. Then I took off my shorts, put my things away, and jumped in the pool to join him.

Mrs. Boggs let me and Tommy swim until our fingers were as wrinkled as prunes and our eyes were bright red from the chlorine. Tommy wasn't nearly as good a swimmer as I was, and lost every race, but he could hold his breath for almost a whole minute longer than I could.

And then we went back to our room, put on the fuzzy white robes that were hanging in our closet on silk hangers, and ordered room service. In case you don't know, room service is supper served in your room, and it's brought on a little cart covered in a pressed white linen tablecloth. Tommy and I both ordered cheeseburgers and french fries, and Mrs. Boggs ordered a healthy-looking chicken salad. Our food came on white porcelain plates, kept warm beneath silver domes, and the ketchup and mustard came in tiny glass bottles.

I stared at it in wonder. Who knew that even *ketchup* could be fancy?

Mrs. Boggs was reading a local magazine that had come with our food. "Would you look at that?" she mused. "There's a pop-up modern art museum outside of Memphis. Maybe if we have enough time, we can stop there."

Tommy made a face. "Sounds boring."

She ruffled his hair. "We'll get some culture into you at some point."

"Maybe." Then Tommy pointed at her plate. "What's that weird curly lettuce in your salad?"

Mrs. Boggs stabbed a piece of it with her fork. It looked more like a weed than a piece of lettuce to me. "It's called frisée. Would you like to try it?"

"Heck no." He bounced up and down in his chair. "Mrs. Boggs, have you always lived in your RV?"

I smiled into my napkin. Sometimes conversations with Tommy felt like talking to a Ping-Pong ball.

"No. No, I haven't." Mrs. Boggs sat back in her chair. "Only for about . . . what's it been? Let's see. Five years? Darryl and I used to live just outside Sacramento,

California, near my parents. We had the most glorious raised-bed garden you've ever seen."

"Why'd you move?" Tommy asked.

"Because we had dreams. The first dream was to have children, but that wasn't in the cards for us. And our second dream was to travel, but we'd never really had the means. And then about six years ago, he invested in his cousin's business. That was Darryl: always helping everyone out, investing in their ideas, even when we couldn't quite afford it. But this time, it paid off. We made quite a bit of money. So we bought the RV and moved out of our house. We planned to drive to the Rocky Mountains of Canada and to the tip of the Baja Peninsula, in Mexico. I couldn't wait. The day we signed the paperwork for the Winnebago was the freest day of my life."

Mrs. Boggs had a sad smile on her face. Her eyes were clouded over like she was looking inside instead of out. "But it wasn't meant to be. Darryl died the week before we were supposed to leave California. Pancreatic cancer, stage four. At least it took him quickly."

I wished I was brave enough to reach out and hold her hand. But "I'm sorry" was all I could say.

Mrs. Boggs waved a hand at me, like she was waving off my sympathy.

"I'm sorry, too, Mrs. Boggs," Tommy said. "That's a sad story. So how come you ended up in Davenport?"

"Darryl grew up in Davenport. He left the second he was old enough to drive a car. Which is why I never understood it, but he always told me he wanted to be buried there, so those were the arrangements I made. But I couldn't leave him. I just couldn't. So after he died, I drove the RV from California and I stayed. And I've been there ever since."

We both sat silently, absorbing her story. I poked at my food, not really interested in my french fries or the fancy ketchup anymore.

"I think you should keep on driving," Tommy said after a few moments. "Don't you think Mr. Boggs would have wanted you to go on your big adventure even if he's not here to share it with you?"

Something in Mrs. Boggs went all clenched up again at Tommy's words. "Mr. Boggs is dead, so he doesn't get to have an opinion."

But wasn't Mr. Boggs's opinion from beyond the grave the whole reason she was helping me get to Nashville in the first place? Why could he advise Mrs. Boggs to help me realize *my* dream, but not her own? It didn't make any sense.

Before I could say so, Mrs. Boggs pushed her salad away and stood up. "I'm going to bed. I'm tired. Push the cart outside the room when you're done eating. Good night."

Tommy and I watched her go. Neither of us could find the appetite to finish our cheeseburgers.

We were also so tired out from all the swimming that we barely watched any TV before we turned off the lights and climbed into our beds.

We had been lying in the dark for only a few minutes when Tommy said, "Hey, May?"

"Yeah?"

There was a long pause. "I don't want to make you mad, and I definitely hope this doesn't make you throw up again," he said, "but I think you should probably pick a song to sing. For the contest. It's only a few days away, and I haven't heard you practicing yet."

My heart beat faster. Once again, I imagined myself up on that stage, all alone, in a bright spotlight, the silence of an uncomfortable audience pounding in my ears.

But then I squeezed my eyes shut and tried to imagine myself onstage in that silver-starlight dress. I willed myself to breathe. And then, in a quiet voice, I said, "I know, Tommy. You're right."

"Oh, good." He sounded relieved I wasn't hightailing it to the bathroom to be sick. "I'll help you brainstorm, if you want. What kind of song are you thinking to sing?"

That part, at least, I had decided. "Country."

"Is that your favorite kind of music?"

"No. But country is someone else's favorite kind of

music. Someone important. Someone who's going to be there the day of the contest."

"Huh? What are you talking about?"

The fact that I would be meeting my daddy so soon was bursting out of me, and I worried that if I didn't tell one person, I might tell the whole world instead. "Tommy, can I tell you a secret?"

Tommy sat up in his bed and turned on the light. "Of course. What is it?"

"It's a big secret. You have to promise not to tell Mrs. Boggs or anyone else."

"Okay. I promise."

I felt like I was about to jump off a cliff, but I forced myself to do it anyway. "The real reason I entered this contest is because . . . my daddy will be there. He's one of the judges. It will be the first time I've ever met him."

Tommy was quiet for a long minute. "Wow," he finally said. "That's really something, May."

And so I told Tommy all of it. I stared at the ceiling while I spoke. It was easier that way. I told him how I heard my daddy's voice on the radio only by chance. How I didn't even know what he looked like. How he didn't even know I existed and how nervous I was he wouldn't like me once he did. How badly I hoped he might fall back in love with Momma, because that way my grandfather might see that we were a normal, happy family worth loving. That Momma hadn't made a mistake by having me.

"I've wanted to call in every time he's been on the air, but I never found the courage to do it. I even have the number memorized. Stupid, huh?"

Tommy looked me square in the eyes. "He'd be a fool not to like you."

Something warm and hopeful bloomed in my chest. "You think?"

"I don't think, I *know*." Then he leaned out over the space between our beds with his pinky finger extended. "And I promise that as long as I shall live, I will never tell your secret, Maybelle Lane. To Mrs. Boggs, your momma, or anyone else."

He meant it, too—all of it. I could tell. I reached out to shake his pinky with my own. "Thanks, Tommy."

I had only just turned the lamp back off and settled against my pillows when Tommy said, "Hey, May?"

"Yeah?"

"I hope she changes her mind."

"Who?"

"Mrs. Boggs. About going on her adventure."

"Oh," I said. "Me too."

I closed my eyes. The room was quiet for only a minute.

"Hey, May?"

"Yeah?"

"Thanks for letting me come."

I smiled into the darkness. "You're welcome, Tommy. I'm glad you're here."

I was surprised to find I meant it.

And then, for the first time in a long time, I didn't toss or turn or lie awake for hours. I didn't slip out of bed to go sit by the window and think about how much I missed Momma, or about any other dark thoughts storming in my head. Because there was no storm.

I just closed my eyes and drifted right off to sleep.

CHAPTER 18

I woke a little after five in the morning. Tommy was snoring, and the door to Mrs. Boggs's room was still shut tight. I got up, wrote a note, and slipped out into the long hotel hallway.

Because Tommy was right. It was time for me to finally pick a song. I spent ten minutes roaming around the hotel, trying to find a nice private place where I could think and practice. I settled on an empty conference room with a huge table and swivelly leather chairs.

A song by Hank Williams Jr. was probably my best bet because he was my daddy's favorite singer of all time. If I was able to do it right, I would blow the socks right off his feet. He'd think, "Wow, this young lady here has good taste in music." And then he would feel an instant connection with me and wouldn't be at all shocked when I went up to him and told him I was his daughter.

I tried two of my daddy's favorite songs: "The Conversation" and "If Heaven Ain't a Lot like Dixie." I had heard my daddy play them both on his show so many times I had them memorized. But to say my first attempt at singing Hank Williams Jr. didn't go well would be the understatement of the century.

It was terrible. *I* was terrible.

I recorded my first tries and listened to them after I finished. It took all my willpower not to open up one of the windows and chuck out my tape recorder right then and there. My voice was cold and out of practice. I couldn't get his country warble down. Apparently, my voice was not a country-warbling kind of voice. I tried singing each song over and over again for the better part of an hour, but I wasn't getting any better. I was getting worse.

"Grah!" I yelled in frustration, tugging on my hair so hard it hurt.

I lay down on the floor and put my feet up on the seat of one of the chairs and rocked it back and forth, thinking. It was no use singing a Hank Williams Jr. song for my daddy if I sounded like a set of car brakes that desperately needed oiling. The point was to impress him, not to make him want to shove cotton balls into his ears. I'd sung "Amazing Grace" as my chorus solo, but I couldn't do that for a contest. Talk about unoriginal.

So if it wasn't country music or "Amazing Grace," what would I sing instead?

My favorite kind of music was the kind that took strange sounds and turned them into something beautiful. Like when bands folded electronic beeping or video game noises into their songs, or when people drummed on plastic buckets or metal bowls and made an unexpected tune. But that wasn't appropriate for a singing contest, seeing as I couldn't drum on buckets and the only strange sounds were the ones on my tape recorder. Maybe I could do something like that one day, but not yet.

I also loved the kind of music where it was only the person singing, with no instruments at all. "A cappella" is what Momma called it. Nothing but pure voice. One single sound against a background of quiet. That was something I could do. But what kind of music should it be?

Something I knew like the back of my hand. Something like . . . Momma's song. The idea popped into my head for only a second before I pushed it away. I'd rather eat a handful of nails than sing that song again, considering what had happened last time I'd sung it.

No other answers were falling into my head while I lay there on the floor, so I stood up and went over to the window. Cars and buses were inching along on the street far below me. One of the buses had MISSISSIPPI, BIRTHPLACE OF AMERICA'S MUSIC! written across its side, same as the sign I'd seen the other day. I stared at it.

Even if Momma didn't like to do it, maybe I could

sing the blues. I wasn't trying to get rich or famous from it, I was just trying to impress my daddy. And there was no music I was more familiar with on this earth than the blues, thanks to Momma, so maybe it was worth a try.

I started pacing around the conference room. My first thought was maybe I could try to do a song by Big Maybelle, the famous R&B singer Momma named me after. It only took me the first few lines of "96 Tears" to know it wasn't a good idea. Trying to hit Big Maybelle's deep, gravelly notes made me feel like a kitten playing dress-up as a lion.

The folky twang of the early blues wasn't right for me, either. It would be better for me to do an R&B ballad. Something with some gospel flair to it.

But no matter how much I tried, I couldn't think of a song that was right for *me*. Every song I began to sing—whether it was by Johnny Adams or Etta James—felt like a shoe that didn't quite fit.

As I tried and failed again and again to find a song, my mood grew dark. I couldn't shake the growing feeling that this whole plan was a big mistake. Should I really put my daddy on the spot like that, showing up at his contest? A voice at the back of my brain screamed, *No, don't do it!*

But I also couldn't ignore the yawning hole in the center of my chest. It had always been there, and it had only grown larger since I found my daddy on the radio. For the most part, Momma was the best kind of mother a girl could ever dream of, but I needed more. The lonely, empty hours of my days needed filling. I needed a daddy. *My* daddy.

And here I was, with a golden chance to finally meet him, to impress him with my singing, but I couldn't even choose a song.

What was wrong with me?

* * *

When I came back into the hotel room a little after nine o'clock, Tommy said, "May! Where you been?"

I glared at him. Hadn't he seen the note? "What do you care?"

I felt like a jerk the minute I said it, because I knew I shouldn't be taking it out on Tommy, who had done nothing wrong. Knowing this only made my dark mood even darker.

Mrs. Boggs poked her head through the door connecting our bedrooms. "May," she said. "Watch your tone."

"Fine. Sorry." But it came out in a huffy, not-sorry-at-all sort of way.

"And watch that attitude, too." She frowned and shook her head at Tommy and me. "Both of you, giving me so much grief this morning. Starting to be more trouble than you're worth. Honestly."

I turned to Tommy. "What did *you* do?"

Mrs. Boggs answered for him. "He went down and started using the concierge's computer without permission. Nearly got us all tossed out of the hotel right then and there."

"The one behind the desk? Why'd you do that?"

Tommy shook his head ever so slightly and then tipped his head toward Mrs. Boggs. "No reason." Then he mouthed, *I'll tell you later.*

"Both of you, start packing," Mrs. Boggs said. "It's time for us to get going."

The darkness of my mood started to ebb away once we were back in the RV. We were on the interstate again, but the city faded away quickly, and the view was back to being fields and fields of rolling country, dotted with tractors and cows. I went up and sat next to Mrs. Boggs in my copilot chair and apologized for my rudeness.

At first, she didn't say anything. But then she looked at me out of the corner of her eye and raised an eyebrow. "I do have to admit I'm glad there's a little vim and vinegar hidden down inside you. It will serve you well—when you use it at the right time. You understand?"

I could tell she meant I had used it at the *wrong* time. "Yes, ma'am. It won't happen again."

"Good. Now, do you want to tell me what's wrong?"

I fiddled with the edge of my jean shorts. "I can't seem to find the right song to sing. I want to find a song that feels like *me*."

"I'm sure you'll find it. Just keep looking."

"Yeah. I guess." Then, after a few seconds, I said, "Mrs. Boggs, do you think it's okay if I sing the blues?"

Mrs. Boggs considered me for a long time. "Are you looking for my permission?"

"No. Well, yes."

"It's not my responsibility to tell you that. I think it's fine for you to sing whatever your heart desires, but I only speak for me. I don't speak for anyone else. So go on and use that big beautiful brain of yours and answer the question for yourself. Do any of these blues songs you're thinking of singing represent you? *You*, Maybelle Lane?"

I thought long and hard on it. "Maybe?"

"I'm not sure that's quite good enough."

And she was right. I knew she was. "Maybe" wasn't good enough. And finally I saw how Momma was right, too. The blues were mine to love and listen to, but they weren't mine to take and try to pass on as my own story.

But what song *did* tell my story? Momma's song did, obviously. But that told the story of my stupidity. My thoughtlessness. The story of how I ruined things for Momma and me. And that's not the story I wanted to tell.

I sighed. I'd think about it later.

159

Next I went back to say sorry to Tommy, too. He accepted my apology immediately. He looked more relieved I wasn't angry with him than mad I had been so rude—that's how nice he was about it.

He glanced over his shoulder toward the front of the RV. "Mrs. Boggs, will you turn on some music?"

"I'm enjoying the silence."

"Please?" Tommy begged. "Please, just one song? My ears are bored!"

Even from my spot in the back of the RV, I could hear the deep whoosh of Mrs. Boggs's sigh. She shook her head as she leaned forward to flip the radio on. "*One* song. Then back to quiet contemplation."

"Thank you!" Tommy turned to me. "Now she can't hear us."

I watched curiously as he pulled a folded piece of paper out of his pocket and slid it across the table to me.

"What's this?" I asked.

"Shh," he said, looking over his shoulder again. "It's the reason I was using the computer in the lobby. I wanted to print something out for you. Look."

So I unfolded the sheet of paper. It was a picture of a man. He had tan skin, brown hair peppered with gray at his temples, and blue eyes. His smile was wide, and his teeth were blinding white, like sunbeams of light were shooting out of each and every tooth.

Tommy didn't even have to tell me who it was a picture of. I knew deep in my bones, right then and there.

It was my daddy.

"I searched his name and the radio station. He popped right up."

Tommy didn't say another word as I traced my fingers along my daddy's face. I had his rounded chin, and the shape of his eyes. He was less handsome than I had imagined, and a little older—not in a disappointing way, but in a way that made my stomach flutter because here he was. Real. Alive.

I tried to commit every detail to memory. The pale scar above his left eyebrow. The day-old stubble on his cheeks. The way his smile crooked a little to the left.

Eventually, I found my voice. "Thank you, Tommy."

"Nah," he said, waving his hand at me. "It's no big whoop."

But it was a big whoop to me. I folded the picture up carefully and slid it into my pocket before I came round and gave Tommy a quick peck on the cheek.

He went bright red and smiled from ear to ear. Close up, I could see the bruise on his cheek was starting to fade around the edges.

And as happy as I was to have a picture of my daddy, I was mad at myself, too. I had been all kinds of wrong in my judgment about troublemaking Tommy O'Brien.

"Seeing his face makes me feel a little nervous," I admitted.

"Why?"

How could I explain? He had a face now. And surely he would have an opinion. About me.

"Are you still worried he won't like you?"

I nodded.

That's when I saw the glimmer in Tommy's eye. "What time did you say your daddy's show is on?"

"In the early afternoon. Why?"

Tommy grabbed my wrist to look at my watch. "Is he on the air now?"

"Well, yes, I think, but—"

I tried to explain that we couldn't listen in because of Mrs. Boggs. But Tommy interrupted me. "I have an idea. Do you have a cell phone?"

"Yeah, but it's an old one—"

"Doesn't matter. Where is it?"

I got it from my backpack and handed it to Tommy. He glanced up front like he wanted to make sure Mrs. Boggs wasn't paying attention to us. Satisfied, he motioned for me to follow him into the bathroom.

"What are you thinking?" I asked him, pulling the door shut behind us.

"You said you memorized the radio station's phone number, right? So what is it?"

I recited it without thinking. Then I watched in horror as Tommy punched the numbers into the phone. "Wait a minute. You aren't going to call in, are you?"

"That's exactly what I'm going to do."

He pressed Call. He had it on speakerphone, so I could hear it ringing.

"You can't!" I cried, trying to grab it away. It was a bad idea. An awful idea! What was he thinking, being so bold? But Tommy wouldn't give up the phone.

"Trust me," he said.

My daddy's voice filled up the bathroom. "Hello, WKBC 101.3, you're on the air. Do you have a question for the great Bill Hixon?"

Bill Hixon? Tommy mouthed.

Bill Hixon was a local country star my daddy had on as a guest all the time. "He's a musical guest," I whispered. "Hang up now!"

But he didn't. Tommy lowered his voice so he was talking gruffly. He sounded exactly like an adult. "No, I have a question for both of y'all, actually. My question is, if an old girlfriend of yours had your baby and never said nothing to you, would you want to know about the child? I'm, uh," Tommy said, glancing at me, "asking for a friend."

Both men laughed. Bill Hixon chimed in first. "A 'friend,' sure. Well, if that was the case for me, I wouldn't live long enough to say hello to my unknown child because my wife would have me out back with a shotgun if she found out I was ever unfaithful to her."

Both of them laughed again. Then my daddy piped up. "Ignore this joker. Of course we would want to know. Or, at least, I would. I don't have any children, not yet, anyway"—for some reason, this made Bill Hixon bang on the table and hoot—"but, as I was saying, I would have to imagine there is nothing more precious on God's green earth than a man's own child. I would treasure that baby with all my heart and soul. Wouldn't you agree, Bill?"

"Amen, Fitzy. Couldn't have said it better myself."

"Does that answer your 'friend's' question?" my daddy asked.

Without answering, Tommy hung up the phone and handed it back to me. "Well, there's your answer," he said triumphantly. "He said you were precious. He said he'd treasure you! Didn't you hear him, May? Why don't you look happier about it?"

Of course I had heard him, but something was chewing on me. Something about the way my daddy had been laughing. It was . . . emptier than normal. It didn't have any of its usual power, the power that always brightened the space around me.

It made me think about how every Wednesday, Gram played bridge with her church ladies. Susan, Kathy, and

Jean, if I'm remembering their names right. Sometimes Gram would bring me along, and I would watch TV as they played. They were all nice enough, but Kathy was a cheat. She would peek at the other ladies' cards whenever they took a break. And when they started playing again, she would laugh too loudly and for too long at things that weren't funny.

It was the exact same kind of empty laugh I'd just heard coming out of my daddy's mouth. A cheater's laugh.

What if I'd been wrong about this—about him—this whole time? What if he didn't even like kids, and wanted nothing to do with me at all?

I tried to explain it to Tommy, but he shook his head at me. "What does your dad have to do with an old lady who cheats at cards? You're imagining it. Really. It sounded like he was telling the truth to me."

I put my hand to my chest, to try to calm the anxious fluttering of my heart. Maybe Tommy was right. Maybe I *was* imagining it. I chewed my lip and let myself sink into the warm possibility of it.

"You're lucky, you know." Tommy leaned against the mirror. "It sounds like you've got good parents. Both of them, not just one."

He was smiling, but his eyes were sad around the edges.

"You know, Tommy, if there's ever anything you want

165

to talk to me about . . . I'm here. I'll listen. Just like you listened for me."

"Okay. Thanks."

There was a stretch of silence. I had the feeling he wasn't ready to talk to me quite yet. But I'd try again.

"Come on," I said, grabbing his hand. "Let's go finish off my Tootsie Pops."

"But only the orange ones are left. I thought you were saving those for your momma."

"Nah," I lied. "I was saving them for you. Now come on before I change my mind."

CHAPTER 19

Apparently, the rest of the Tootsie Pops didn't fill Tommy up, because no less than an hour beyond Jackson, he announced he was hungrier than a hippopotamus.

We were bumping and rolling along I-55, with flashing signs letting us know we had passed the small town of Winona and would soon be entering Grenada.

Mrs. Boggs flicked her eyes to look at Tommy in the rearview mirror. "It's only another hour or so until Memphis. Can it wait?"

"I guess so," Tommy said mournfully.

I patted my stomach. I'd missed the hotel's breakfast buffet because I had been practicing my singing, which had sucked me dry. In fact, my head and my heart both felt just as empty and sharp as my stomach did. "Actually, Mrs. Boggs, I'm hungry, too."

"Yes!" Tommy cried, pumping his fist in the air. "Two against one. Hey . . . we could go there!"

He pointed at a faded billboard coming toward us on the side of the interstate. It said HENRY'S HOT DOG HEAVEN, 2 MILES OFF EXIT 206.

"Please, can we get hot dogs?" Tommy asked. "Please, please, please . . ."

"Hot dogs aren't food. Nothing but rubbery bits of toxic waste, if you ask me." But she clicked on her right blinker to exit off the interstate anyway.

Henry's Hot Dog Heaven was a small white building at the center of a big parking lot. Mrs. Boggs could have parked the RV sideways across ten parking spots had she wanted to, because there wasn't a single other car there.

As we walked across the steaming hot parking lot, I half expected a tumbleweed to come bouncing along with a low whistle of wind. *That's* how empty it felt.

"Do you think it's open?" I asked.

"Says so on the door," Mrs. Boggs replied.

A bell tinkled as we went in. The restaurant was as old and tired as its billboard. I wrinkled my nose. It smelled less like hot dogs and more like rotten eggs.

A bald, red-faced man had appeared behind the counter, with an apron on and a rag thrown over his shoulder. He had deep creases on his forehead and around his eyes, which made him look angry even when he smiled.

"Welcome to Henry's Hot Dog Heaven. I'm Henry. Can I help y'all?"

"Yes. We want some hot dogs," Tommy said.

"Fine. Take a seat in that booth over there. I'll get you some menus." He was going toward the back when he muttered, "You hear that, Pickle? You better behave."

Tommy, Mrs. Boggs, and I eyed each other as we slid into a booth. There was no one else in the restaurant.

Henry brought some laminated menus and three plastic cups filled with water. Tommy and I both ordered Cokes, while Mrs. Boggs took a meaningful sip of water and said something under her breath about all the preservatives and chemicals in soda pop. We ignored her.

"They've got chili cheese dogs," Tommy said, once Henry left to get our drinks. "And double dogs. And corn dogs! And—*what the*—vegetarian dogs? How's that possible? And bacon dogs—"

And that's when it happened. It was a quiet squeak, but it was an unmistakable sound. The rotten egg smell crept into my nostrils, ten times stronger than when we first walked in. I needed a gas mask, *that's* how bad it was. Tommy stopped talking mid-sentence and looked up from the menu. It didn't take long for his contagious giggles to bubble up.

There was only one explanation: someone had farted. And judging from Tommy's reaction, it wasn't him. Which

169

only left one person, because it certainly wasn't me. I was so embarrassed for Mrs. Boggs, Tommy's contagious giggles didn't even make me smile.

Tommy nudged her with his elbow. "Did you eat beans for breakfast, Mrs. Boggs?"

She didn't seem to get the joke. "What? No. I had some rye toast and yogurt."

Henry appeared at our table with our Cokes and to take our orders. A vegetarian dog for Mrs. Boggs, two chili cheese dogs for Tommy, and a corn dog with extra honey mustard for me. He was about to go back into the kitchen when he stopped and sniffed the air.

"God darn it, Pickle. What did I *just* say?" He grabbed a spoon from our table and flung it toward the underside of the counter. We heard it clatter, followed by a yelp and a whimper.

Mrs. Boggs bent over to see what—or who—had whimpered. When she looked back at Henry, her eyes were glittering and sharp. "Is that a poor little dog you threw my spoon at, or is that my imagination?"

I craned my neck to see for myself. It *was* a dog. A small wiener dog, cowering behind one of the counter-top stools.

"It sure is a dog. A no-good one at that."

As if on cue, the poor dog farted again. Tommy didn't laugh this time around.

Before I could stop myself, I blurted out, "You shouldn't talk to him like that. Can't you see he's scared?"

"Oh, he's scared? I'll tell you who's scared: all my customers are scared. No one will come eat here anymore because of this disgusting creature. I've been meaning to sell him on the internet, but I haven't had the time. Doubt I could even give away this dog for free."

Given the raggedy look of the place, I doubted his lack of customers had anything to do with that sweet little dog. I was about to say so, but Tommy jumped to his feet and beat me to it.

"Oh yeah? If he's such a pest to you, then *we'll* take him."

"Let's all settle down," Mrs. Boggs said quickly, eyeing Tommy. "I'm not sure adding a dog to the mix is such a great idea."

I stood up. "No. Tommy's right, Mrs. Boggs. We should take him with us." I glanced meaningfully at Tommy, whose hands were balled up into two tight, white-knuckled fists. "Because *no one* should have to live somewhere where the person who's supposed to take care of them hurts them. It's not the way it's supposed to be."

The look on Mrs. Boggs's face changed. "You know what? You're right, May. You're exactly right." She reached into her pocketbook and pulled out a crisp twenty-dollar bill.

I could see the cogs turning in Henry's head. "Two hundred, and he's yours. Heck, I'll even throw in lunch."

"But you just said you were going to give him away for free!" I cried.

"The price has changed," he said, eyeing the money in Mrs. Boggs's hand.

Mrs. Boggs's lips pressed together even tighter. "Why don't you go make our hot dogs and we'll think it over."

Henry laughed. It wasn't a nice or joyful sound. "Fine. Doesn't matter to me."

He went back to the kitchen, and as I watched him go, my hunger disappeared. Suddenly the idea of a corn dog made by *that* man seemed as appealing as a slimy frog-leg sandwich.

"I don't know about you two," Mrs. Boggs said, crumpling up her napkin, "but I've lost my appetite."

"Me too," Tommy said.

"May," Mrs. Boggs said, putting her hand on my shoulder. "Why don't you go and see if you can coax the poor thing out. I have a feeling he'll respond to your quiet nature." She flicked her eyes toward the kitchen. "And be quick about it, won't you?"

I gaped at her. "You don't mean we're going to *take* him, do you?"

"That is exactly what I mean. You were right, in what you said before. This dog does deserve a better life, and it shouldn't cost us two hundred dollars to give it to him. I'll get the RV powered up. Tommy, wait here with May. Keep a lookout."

Heart thumping, I went over to where the dog was hiding and bent down. "Here, doggy, doggy."

Two big brown eyes peeked out at me from beneath silver eyebrows. When he crawled forward, I could see he was wearing a dirty, saggy diaper.

I got onto my knees and clicked my tongue, putting my hand out toward him so he could sniff it. "Here, Pickle. Here, doggy, doggy. I'm not gonna hurt you."

He inched out toward me. It took me a long second to realize why he was moving so funny: his back legs weren't working. He was dragging them along the cold linoleum floor. I swear, my heart grew two sizes right then and there. "It's okay. I won't hurt you. I promise."

"Hurry, May," Tommy said, bouncing nervously on his heels. "I think I hear him coming."

Pickle's tail started thumping hesitantly. I took that as a good sign, so I reached out and scooped him up into my arms.

And then I ran.

"Hey!" It was Henry, coming out of the kitchen. "Hey, what do you think you're doing! Stop right there!"

Mrs. Boggs was waiting outside with the RV rumbling and its door wide open. We jumped in and she peeled off so quickly, we barely got the door closed behind us. Tommy and I watched out the window as Henry threw his dishrag onto the pavement and went back inside. I hugged Pickle closer to me.

Even though he stank worse than old cheese, I knew those pains in my heart had to be love.

* * + * *

Poor Pickle was a nervous wreck. We all were. I kept expecting to hear the *whoop-whoop* of police sirens behind us, but once we had driven twenty minutes beyond Henry's Hot Dog Heaven and there was still no one on our tail, I started to relax.

The first thing I did was take off the crusty old diaper Pickle had been forced to wear. Henry must have put it on him so he didn't even have to take him outside to do his business.

I plugged my nose, peeled it off, and then I got started checking on his back legs. They were much weaker and skinnier than his front legs, and the places where the diaper had rubbed against him were red and raw-looking. His stomach was all bloated out, too, the way Momma's got whenever she ate too much dairy. Pickle quivered and trembled beneath my fingers, even though I was gentle as could be.

Tommy knelt down next to me and held his nose

between his thumb and forefinger. "Pee-yew. He stinks to high heaven. What's wrong with his back legs?"

"I don't know. They don't seem to work."

"So he just drags himself around?"

"I think so."

Tommy had a look on his face like he was thinking hard about something. "Huh. That can't feel good. I wonder if he's paralyzed, like my aunt's dog."

"I don't know. I hope not. Mrs. Boggs!" I called out. "Would you mind stopping before we get to Memphis? I want to give Pickle a bath, but I'm afraid the water will slosh out all over the floor if I do it while we're moving."

"Yeah, and stop in one of those Walmart parking lots," Tommy added. "I got some shopping I wanna do."

"You *have* some shopping you *want* to do," Mrs. Boggs corrected him.

She also said she was tired out anyway, something about the hotel's mattress being too soft, so we stopped for the night at a Walmart in Batesville, which was still a full hour away from Memphis (or more like two, with Mrs. Boggs driving).

As soon as we parked, both Mrs. Boggs and Tommy went into the Walmart, leaving me and Pickle alone in the RV. I gave Tommy the old diaper to throw away so Pickle would never have to see that dirty thing ever again.

I filled up the sink with warm, sudsy water and cooed at Pickle while he quivered and quaked beneath the dining table. He was passing wind again. I was starting to think it was some kind of a nervous tic.

When I picked him up and put him gently in the water, his shaking got even worse.

"Shhh," I said. "It's okay. I got you. I won't let go."

Pickle whimpered and pawed frantically at the edge of the sink. It made my heart ache to think of the awful way this poor dog must have been treated in his life to be so scared of a warm bath.

I wished I'd thought to record the jingle of the bell on the hot dog restaurant's door when we walked in—it was the sound of Pickle's fate changing, the sound of the three of us coming to whisk him away. But at the time, I didn't know it was important. That's why you should always pay attention to the details around you, no matter how small they may be. Because they might just change your life.

Pickle shook beneath my fingertips. How could I make him understand his life would be filled with love and tenderness from now on? I tried shushing him, cooing at him, scratching him behind his velvety ears, but none of it worked. He was quaking so violently, I feared the poor dog's heart was going to stop right then and there.

When I was littler, Momma's song was the only thing that calmed me down after a bad nightmare or a skinned knee. Maybe that would be Pickle's truth, too. I had to try something for that poor dog, and this was the best thing I had. So, as I scrubbed away the dirt and the loneliness from his fur, I sang.

"She came to me on a cold, dark night. . . ."

I stopped singing and squeezed my eyes closed before I even finished the first line. It felt all wrong, the words painful in my throat instead of soothing. Images of my grandfather staring at me like I was a stranger flooded back into my head, his words ringing in my ears. *Maybelle. What are you doing here?* Momma crumpled over crying on the couch when she learned we had to move. Gram crying, too. The same old thoughts whirligigging through my brain.

If only I hadn't been singing. If only I had made no noise at all.

But then I felt something cold and wet nudging my fingers. Pickle's nose. It took me a second to realize his shaking had quieted down. He was looking up at me with his big brown eyes, and it made my shoulders relax and my heart beat at a more even pace. So I closed my eyes and ignored the worry and the memories and the dread, and I let the words flow out.

She came to me on a cold, dark night
The stars hidden behind my closed eyes

The darkness felt like home
But I had to open up and let go

They don't get you ready for this love

My baby, the stars
My baby, the moon
The universe told me to surrender
It told me to

Said you'd light the way, so I opened my eyes
And the starlight came flooding in

Yeah, my baby will light the way
I know, I know it will be okay

My baby will light the way back home

My baby, the stars
My baby, the moon
The universe told me to surrender
It told me to.

When I finished, Pickle leaned his head back and let out a long, low howl. He wasn't shaking anymore, not even a little bit, *and* he was clean.

I pulled the plug in the sink. Something heavy and dark I had been holding on to for a long, long time seemed to disappear right down the drain with the soapy water.

A new lightness took its place.

As the much calmer Pickle shook out his fur, spraying me with droplets of doggy-scented water, everything clicked into place. There was no other song I was meant to sing up on that stage in Nashville.

Because this song told my story. Sure, it made me remember how I was a stupid girl who made a huge mistake and said too much to her grandfather.

But I was also a girl who calmed a broken dog. A girl with a mother who loved her dearly. Maybe I could be all those things at once. And maybe that was okay. Because this song was me. The pain, but also the love.

I reached out and hugged Pickle close, wet fur and all. I laughed as he licked my face.

Even if my grandfather couldn't open his heart toward me and Momma, maybe my daddy could. Maybe he'd hear my story and understand I was worth loving after all.

CHAPTER 20

Tommy appeared ten minutes later with plastic bags hitched up to his elbows. He tilted his head at me. "Something about you seems different."

"I chose a song," I said proudly.

He slid into the booth and put the plastic bags on the table. "Cool! Will you sing it for me?"

"No," I said. "It's not ready yet."

Of course, that wasn't the full truth. I knew Momma's song inside out and could sing it hanging upside down from a jungle gym with my eyes closed. It was *me* who wasn't ready yet. I could sing it in front of Pickle, sure, but he was a dog. Tommy was a person. And the sea of people staring at me from the audience— they would all be living, breathing people, too. I needed time before I was ready for that. I petted Pickle. His warm body on my lap made me feel a little better somehow.

As Mrs. Boggs started making an early supper, Tommy unpacked his Walmart purchases onto the table. It was the strangest assortment of things I ever did see.

He had a set of training wheels—the kind you add to a kid's bike—a few rolls of ribbon, some plastic pipes, a pair of women's spandex shorts, duct tape, a set of screws, a nice red leash, and a screwdriver.

When I asked him what it was all for, Tommy was mysterious about it. He only waggled his eyebrows at me. "You'll see."

He started taking apart the training wheels with the screwdriver. The table quickly turned into a workshop, and Mrs. Boggs didn't even make Tommy clean it up while we ate. She cooked a stir-fry for us humans and made white rice and plain boiled chicken for Pickle, which he gobbled right up.

She nodded at his bloated stomach. "That's a sore stomach, if ever I did see one. I had two dogs growing up, and this is always what we fed them whenever they weren't feeling well."

About an hour after dinner, Tommy finished his mystery project. "Grab Pickle and bring him outside, would you, May?"

Pickle was underneath the table, gnawing happily on

181

the edge of one of the cardboard boxes full of Mr. Boggs's old stuff. I gathered Pickle under one arm and quickly swiveled the box so Mrs. Boggs wouldn't notice the damage. I'd have to teach him not to do that.

The parking lot was mostly empty by now, but the heat of the day still lingered on its black pavement. "Here," I said, handing Pickle over to Tommy. Almost immediately, the dog started quivering and passing gas again.

"It's all right, I'm not gonna hurt you," he said, placing Pickle into the contraption he'd made.

Tommy had used the wheels and the plastic pipes to form a little doggy scooter. He had cut up the spandex shorts to make a sort of sling, so the back half of Pickle's body would be lifted up off the ground. So now, instead of having to drag his back legs along the floor, he would be able to *roll*. I jumped up and down and clapped. "Oh, Tommy, you're a genius!"

"Let's see if it works first," he said, breathing through his mouth. "Dang, his farts stink."

Pickle continued to tremble as Tommy strapped him in. Even Mrs. Boggs had taken her nose out of her book and followed us outside to see what was happening.

Once Pickle was secured, Tommy carefully placed him on the pavement. Pickle stood frozen solid for a good minute, then he started growling and biting at the training wheels. But you could see it play out on his face as it dawned on him what the wheels were for. Because he took a step forward. And then another. And soon enough, he was running. He ran in wide loops around the RV at breakneck speed, his long ears flapping as he went. I had the sense he was running for the simple joy of it. He stopped every now and then to lift his head and howl.

"Tommy!" I clapped my hands together. "You're amazing! The scooter works! How'd you know how to make that?"

"It's not a scooter. It's a wheelchair. My dad made one exactly like this for my aunt's dog last year, when he hurt his spine and couldn't use his back legs anymore," Tommy explained. "My dad's good at fixing stuff. When he's not out on his truck routes, we do projects together. He showed me how he did it. I'm just glad I remembered how." Tommy watched Pickle running. "Hopefully it will help his stomach, too. Once my aunt's dog had his, he started going to the bathroom normally again."

Mrs. Boggs patted Tommy on the shoulder. "You've shown great kindness in the service you provided for that dog. You should be proud of yourself. Darryl would say you've got the real makings of an engineer."

"Really?" Tommy asked. "You really think so?"

Mrs. Boggs nodded. "I really do."

Tommy blushed. "I've been reading his old textbooks.

I'm glad you kept them. And I'm glad you made us choose a book to read."

"Me too," I added, nodding. I'd already finished *The Wonderful Wizard of Oz* and started it all over again. I liked rereading books better than going through them the first time, because I liked knowing how the stories would end better than being surprised. I especially liked knowing that in the end, the Cowardly Lion would find his courage, and Dorothy, her way back home. I only wished I could know the ending to my own story, though I supposed life didn't exactly work that way.

Only a couple of minutes after we'd all gone back inside, Pickle trotted to the RV door, lifted his head, and howled.

I nudged Tommy with my shoulder. "He loves it so much, he wants to go outside again!"

Mrs. Boggs glanced over at Pickle. "That, or he's got some business to take care of. Come on, boy."

When Mrs. Boggs took Pickle back outside, I looked at Tommy. I thought about the quick way he'd tried to fix my pocket radio and how easily he could explain how all the pieces of Mrs. Boggs's digital alarm clock worked. I couldn't believe I'd been blind to it for so long.

"You are a genius, aren't you, Tommy?"

He ran his hand through his hair. "Nah, I'm no genius. I just like to build stuff, that's all."

"That's not true." I pointed at Mr. Boggs's engineering textbook. With Mrs. Boggs's permission, Tommy had made some notes for himself in the margins. "People who 'just like to build stuff' don't read books like that. How come you're always getting in trouble at school?"

Tommy shrugged. "I dunno. I get bored, I guess." Then he grinned. "Can you imagine how shocked Principal LaMer would be if he heard you calling *me* a genius? I bet his eyes would bug out of his skull."

I smiled. "Maybe they would. But it wouldn't make it any less true. My momma says smart comes in all shapes and sizes."

"And isn't that the truth," Mrs. Boggs said, coming back inside with Pickle. Once Mrs. Boggs set him down, Pickle came running over to me, yapping happily. His stomach already looked less bloated. "This dog was finally able to relieve himself, thanks to your invention, Tommy. I think he's been holding it all on the inside."

I soon learned his stomach wasn't completely better, because I let him sleep curled up in my arms, and all night, he farted like he wasn't a tiny little dog, but a humongous rhinoceros. He snored like one, too. I hardly got a wink of sleep, due to the sounds and the smells, but I suppose you learn to live with these things when you love somebody.

CHAPTER 21

The next day, we passed the Tennessee state line. The welcome sign was not nearly as interesting to me as Mississippi's was, but this time around, I realized, I *was* starting to feel different.

Mrs. Boggs was growing more comfortable with driving the RV, so we reached Memphis in record time. By her slow standards, that is. Tommy begged and begged Mrs. Boggs to stop at Graceland, the home of the leg-shaking rock 'n' roll star Elvis Presley, and so we did.

Once we got there, we found out the tickets were expensive and no dogs were allowed, so I volunteered to stay behind with Pickle. I wasn't all that interested in Elvis, so I didn't mind. Plus, the weather was hotter and muggier than on the past three days combined—I was grateful to stay inside in the chilly air-conditioning. Mrs. Boggs had it on so blissfully low, I had to drape a blanket around my shoulders.

I was also grateful for a chance to practice singing in private. Every time I began, I felt a shiver of worry go up my spine that I wouldn't be able to finish it. But I did. It helped that Pickle howled when I finished, like it was his own doggy version of applause.

Even though I felt more confident every time I ran through the song, questions still burbled in my brain, nagging at me. I couldn't stop thinking about the way my daddy had laughed on the radio. My thoughts were playing tug-of-war with each other: My daddy's kind words about me being precious. Tommy saying it sounded like the truth to him. Momma's warning that my daddy was bad news, that he would only break my heart. My hope to know him. My fear he wouldn't want to know me.

I couldn't help but think of *The Wonderful Wizard of Oz*. All those characters had found what they were looking for. Would I?

The storm of my thoughts quieted down once Mrs. Boggs and Tommy were back from the tour of Elvis's house. Tommy wouldn't stop firing finger guns at me and saying, "Hey, li'l momma, thank you, thank you very much," in a funny Elvis accent. I made him say a few different things so I could get a recording of him.

"Maybe I'll be an Elvis impersonator when I grow

up," he said. He wiggled the ends of Pickle's ears. "You ain't nothin' but a hound dog. . . ."

I laughed. He *was* pretty good at it. At the Graceland gift shop, he had bought himself a pair of sparkly Elvis sunglasses and had used a black marker to draw long sideburns on the sides of his face.

"If you get so much as a smudge of ink on my linens, heaven help you," Mrs. Boggs said once she saw him.

Mrs. Boggs said she felt energized, so she kept on driving instead of taking her afternoon rest. The highway passed mostly through forest and farmland, with only a couple of stores dotting the sides of the road here and there. We passed a store for cowboys, and one selling fresh-made jams and country hams. A small sign announced we were on the Music Highway.

By three p.m., we were approaching the city limits of Nashville, Tennessee. Our final destination. Mrs. Boggs was mighty pleased with herself, because she'd made the drive faster than she thought she would. It was Friday, and the contest wasn't until Sunday evening.

"This gives us all of Saturday to explore Nashville and get ourselves settled. It all worked out perfectly, now, didn't it?"

"Yes, ma'am," I replied.

And of course, that's exactly when everything started to go wrong.

This one came out of nowhere. The worst ones always did.

We were on the highway, almost within Nashville's city limits, when I felt it.

It was like a fist was tightening around my heart. My breaths were coming out in short, shallow bursts as it squeezed tighter and tighter. The pressure got so bad I started having trouble breathing.

It wasn't just one of my attacks. I was dying. I was actually dying this time.

A storm began to roar inside my head. The walls of the RV started closing in on me. I couldn't move, I couldn't stand, I couldn't breathe. I wasn't getting enough air. I crumpled from the couch onto the floor, clutching my chest.

Tommy was kneeling next to me in a flash. "May? May, are you okay?"

I can't breathe, I tried to say, but no words came out. The world was starting to go dark, except for small bursts of white light.

This was it. But I wasn't ready. The fear was icy cold, and it was everywhere.

I don't want to die, I thought. *I don't want to die, I don't want to die, I don't want to die. . . .*

"Mrs. Boggs!" Tommy cried. "Stop the RV! Something's wrong with Maybelle!"

His words floated up over me. I was at the bottom of a deep, dark well, and he was shouting from the very top.

Again, like it was coming from very far away, I heard the whine of brakes and the honking of horns as the RV came to a stop. Then my vision filled up with the sight of Mrs. Boggs's worried face.

"It's all right, May," she said. "I want you to breathe; breathe with me. Deep from your belly, like this"—she sucked air in deep and slow—"like you've got a balloon in there. And then blow it out, long and slow."

I tried to copy her, but every breath I took was too shallow. It wasn't enough. I still wasn't getting enough air.

"What's wrong with her?" Tommy cried. "Tell me!"

"She's having a panic attack. Her mom said this might happen." Her tone was gentle but firm. She cupped my face with her hands. "Breathe, May. Long and slow. I'm here with you. I'm not going anywhere. I won't let anything bad happen to you, I promise. But I need you to breathe with me, long and slow." She continued to breathe deeply. In, then out. In, then out.

After what felt like an eternity, I started to breathe again. In, then out. In, then out. But by the time I had regained control of my lungs, I was shaking worse than Pickle, and my face was wet with tears.

"That's good, May," Mrs. Boggs said. "You got it. Keep on breathing, just like that." Before I could protest, she gathered me into her arms and lifted me up with a strength I didn't know she had. She carried me into her bedroom in the back of the RV and tucked me into her bed.

I tried to say I was fine, I was okay, I didn't mean to impose, but she shushed me and tucked the covers in tightly around me. "You rest," she said. "Don't worry about anything. Close your eyes and try to sleep."

I managed to get out one word. "Pickle."

A minute later, I felt Pickle's soft, warm body being placed next to me on the bed. He shimmied forward and licked my face before he settled in, curling up right in the crook of my neck. He couldn't have gotten himself any closer.

And then I slept.

It was nighttime when I woke up. From what I could see out the window, it looked like we were in some sort of wide parking area.

I lay there for a while and stared at the ceiling. The thing about panic attacks is that you can't always guess when they're going to hit. You can be sucking on your favorite kind of Popsicle on a perfect summer's day, feeling great, when—*wham!*—it hits you out of nowhere. It's like you're nothing but an old soda pop can and the world is an angry giant, trying to crunch you beneath its heel. Even if you've survived them dozens of times, it doesn't change the fact that when they start, you *know* you're about to die, like it's the only truth left in this world. And then, when you come out on the other side, you feel stupid and embarrassed and ashamed for making such a big deal out of nothing.

The first time it happened was about a month after we moved to Davenport. Momma sped the entire way to the emergency room with a wild look on her face. "Hold on, May," she kept saying. "Just hold on."

I had calmed down enough so I could talk again once we were in the exam room. The doctor listened to my heart, checked my eyes with a penlight, and asked me to practice breathing in and out so he could listen to my lungs.

Everything seemed okay, he said. He asked me a few more questions about my sleeping habits and if I worried about things and stuff like that before he took off his glasses and held my hand between his. I can still remember how warm his palms were. "Have you been through anything stressful recently, little girl?"

Momma was biting her lip like she was about to start crying. I knew I had to at least *try* to be brave, for her sake.

"No, sir," I said, squaring my shoulders. "Nothing at all."

For some reason, this made Momma cry anyway. She

cried while she told the doctor about how we had recently moved. She kept on crying while the doctor talked about "anxiety" and "coping strategies" and gave us a stack of pamphlets. Momma cried the whole way home.

"I'm so sorry," she kept saying, even though *I* was the one who should have been sorry.

Momma told me I should always call her if I had one again when she was at work and she'd come straight home, no questions asked. The worrying that it would happen again was so bad, it was almost a relief when the next one came. Except, of course, it wasn't. I called Momma, like she said to, and she dropped everything and came straight home. She sat on the couch with me all night, playing her guitar and singing happy songs, telling me it would be okay. What she didn't tell me was that by coming home in the middle of her shift, she almost lost her job. I only found that out after I overheard her talking on the phone with a co-worker about how angry her manager had been.

After that, I stopped calling when it happened. I couldn't be the reason she got fired. She had enough on her plate, and I couldn't be the one to ruin things for us. *Again.*

I sighed and rubbed my face. Pickle was still curled up next to me on the pillow, snoring away. I slipped out of the room without waking him.

Tommy and Mrs. Boggs were playing some kind of card game at the dining table when I came in. Tommy jumped to his feet when he saw me, scattering his cards everywhere. "May! You're awake! I'm so glad you're okay. You scared me. Are you feeling better?"

"A little," I said. I looked at Mrs. Boggs, who was watching me carefully. "Thank you for your kindness earlier, ma'am. I'm sorry for all the trouble. I haven't had one of those in a while, so I wasn't expecting it."

Mrs. Boggs put her cards down on the table and came over to me. And that's when she did something unexpected: she hugged me.

But she didn't feel stiff as a board this time. It was a real hug. The kind Momma or Gram would give me, a hug full of love that invites you in. She rocked me back and forth, as comforting as a porch swing.

"I'm so sorry," I said again.

Mrs. Boggs pulled back and held my shoulders. "May. Do you mind having to give Pickle a bath?"

"No. Of course not."

"Do you mind feeding him? Or cuddling him? Or making him feel better when he's afraid?"

I shook my head again.

"Does it maybe make you feel a little bit *good* to do these things for him?"

"Yes," I said. Because it did. It felt better than anything.

"See? You don't have to say you're sorry, because it's okay to let the people who care about you take care of you sometimes. If not for you, then for us."

There was truth to her words. I did like taking care of Pickle. In fact, I loved it. I even liked taking care of Momma, in the little ways I could. I guess it made sense that other people might like taking care of me, too.

But the warm feeling her words gave me didn't last for too long.

"Thank you," I said. Mrs. Boggs gave me one last squeeze before she let go. "But there's something I need to tell you."

"What's that?"

"I . . ." It felt like a lump of sharp rock was sitting in my throat. I forced myself to swallow. "I can't do it."

"You can't do what?"

"I can't sing in that contest. I thought I could do it, but I can't. I'm sorry I made you come all this way for nothing. I want to go home."

CHAPTER 22

Mrs. Boggs didn't try to talk me out of it, even though Tommy yelled out, "What? No! You can't!" Mrs. Boggs shushed him with a hand on his shoulder, and then she gave me one of her soul-searching stares. "Are you sure?"

I was.

Because who did I think I was? I couldn't even cross the state line of Tennessee without falling to pieces. I thought about what would happen if I panicked onstage. Someone in the crowd would probably call an ambulance. There'd be a big scene. And then, when they all realized I was completely fine and had made a big something out of nothing, people would murmur behind their hands, embarrassed for me. And even if I got to meet my daddy after all that, what could I possibly say? "Hi,

I'm your daughter, and I've got a whole bunch of issues. Aren't you happy to meet me?"

And then at the end of all of it, Momma would be stuck with a big fat hospital bill.

I was fooling myself to think I could ever possibly make this plan work.

At least I could stop worrying about the not knowing. Now I knew the ending to this part of my story: it wouldn't be with me and my daddy meeting in Nashville.

So I nodded. "I'm sure."

"And you won't regret it?" Mrs. Boggs asked.

The sound of my daddy's night-sky voice rang in my ears, followed by the image of his big, white-toothed smile flashing in my mind. I did my best to force those thoughts out of my head.

"No," I said. "I won't regret it. I promise."

She stared at me like she was trying to see inside my skull. Finally, she nodded. "Well, okay. If you're sure. We'll turn around first thing tomorrow morning. And, May," she added, "your mother called. I promised her you would call her back as soon as you woke up."

I picked at a stray thread coming loose from the hem of my shirt. "Did you tell her about my attack?"

"Yes, I did."

"Okay," I said, trying not to wince. I wished she hadn't said anything. It would only worry Momma, especially since she was far away and there was nothing she could do about it.

"Make sure to tell her about our change of plans, too."

I nodded, grabbed my phone, and then headed back into Mrs. Boggs's room, shutting the door behind me.

It was heavenly to hear Momma's voice. Apparently, the guests loved her so much, she was asked to give extra performances even when she wasn't scheduled. And then it was even more heavenly to hear that, because of unexpected stormy weather in the Bahamas, the last cruise she was scheduled to go out on for her contract got canceled.

"The last three nights the ship was rocking back and forth so much, most people couldn't eat even the smallest bite of food, me included," Momma said. "It's looking like we'll be back in Miami tonight, and then we've got to stay there for a crew debriefing for the next three to four days. I should be home by the end of the week."

Those were some of the sweetest words I'd ever heard. I didn't get a chance to say how happy that made me, because she didn't want to talk about her. She wanted to know about me. "Are you sure you're okay? Really, really okay? I can't believe I'm not there to be with you through this. I'm so sorry, May. Are you worried about the contest? Is that what triggered it?"

"Maybe," I said. "I don't know."

"Have I told you recently how proud I am of you for doing this? Because I am. You inspire me. Thinking of you being brave gives me strength, too, you know."

I leaned my forehead against the RV's wall and closed my eyes. Now was the time to tell her I wasn't going to sing. That I was a no-good, scaredy-cat quitter. But when I opened my mouth to tell her, that's not what came out.

"Why does my granddaddy hate me so much?" I took a deep breath. "Is it because you weren't married when I was born?"

I'd always imagined it like some sort of stain. Like the doctor came out into the hospital waiting room and, instead of my birth certificate, he handed out a card that had *MISTAKE* written on it in big, black letters, a card that would forever be attached to me. "I'm sorry," I imagined the doctor saying to my grandparents. "I am so sorry."

"Hate you? He doesn't hate you. Not at all. Is that what you've been thinking all this time? That he hates you because I wasn't married when you were born?"

"Maybe."

"Oh, May. His problem is with me, not with you. Things have always been complicated between us. He's never approved of me or my life choices. I believe in God, but not in church. I believe in love, and I've always felt love toward every kind of person, regardless of their gender.

And I think it's perfectly okay to have beautiful babies even if you aren't married." She paused for a long minute. "Did you know that when you were born, he tried to convince me to let him and my mother raise you?"

The news was like a wallop to the head. My grandfather had wanted to *raise* me?

"He . . . did?"

"He did," Momma replied. "He wanted to legally adopt you. He thought if he and your gram raised you, he'd be able to save you from my 'sins.' But I took one look at your perfect baby hands and your perfect baby feet and I knew you didn't need a single lick of saving. And you know what? Neither did I. I'd never give you up for anything, May. Never."

"But . . . but I still don't understand," I told her. "If he was willing to raise me, adopt me, then how come he doesn't ever want to see me?"

"He said if that was my choice, to keep you, he didn't want a relationship with either of us. He thought I'd bring you up wrong-minded. Some people have trouble accepting people that make different choices than they do, even when they're family. *Especially* when they're family." She paused, then said, "Baby. Listen good now. The hardness of my father's heart is not a knock against you. It's a knock against him and him alone. He's the one who's missing out."

I'd never heard Momma sound so strong or so sure.

"But doesn't it hurt?"

"Of course it hurts. It hurts terribly. But the love and joy I get from my relationship with *you* more than makes up for it."

I didn't have much else to say after that. I felt drained of words and thoughts and everything else, so I said the only thing still left inside me. "I love you, Momma."

"I love you, too. More than anything in this world."

CHAPTER 23

Mrs. Boggs decided that we would spend the night in the parking lot. It was wide and empty, so Tommy and I took some peanut butter and jelly sandwiches outside and let Pickle run around off his leash.

He zipped back and forth, stopping only long enough to catch his breath and howl his joy. That doggy sure liked to run. I bet it felt good, after not being able to for so long. His gas attacks were getting better by the hour. He was healing.

While we watched Pickle get some exercise, Tommy kept trying to talk me out of my decision. He knocked a long stick against the side of the RV and wouldn't look at me. "But what about your daddy?"

I took a bite of my sandwich and shrugged. "What about him?"

"You've got this amazing chance to finally meet him, and you're wasting it."

I didn't respond. I didn't really want to talk about this anymore.

"But I don't get it," Tommy pressed. "Your daddy said he would want to know you. He said you were a treasure, live on air, with thousands of people listening in."

"So?"

"So why are you so scared?"

Now *I* wished I had a stick to knock and bang. How on earth could I explain it to him? How badly I wanted to stop being afraid—afraid of the stage, the audience, of what my daddy would say when he found out I existed—but how every time I let myself gain even the tiniest foothold of confidence, a gale of ice-cold wind would come blowing, threatening to knock me down? I wanted to be brave enough to meet my father more than anything I had ever wanted in the whole world. And I loved to sing. Singing was the sound and thrust and feeling of sky-bound joy, and I hated that my fear had taken it away from me.

"I made my decision, and I'm not going to change my mind. Please leave me alone about it, Tommy."

He banged the stick again, hard. It splintered in half and left a long scratch on the side of the Winnebago.

"Hey! Stop that. What's the matter with you?"

"You wouldn't get it."

"Try me."

Tommy snapped the remaining part of the stick in his hands in half and watched the pieces crumble to the ground. "It's that . . . for me . . . things are different. I don't want to go home. Not yet."

Oh, I realized. Of course. Here I'd been so focused on my own problems that I'd forgotten about Tommy's.

"Why not?" I asked.

The question was so fragile I didn't dare move or breathe after asking, because I was scared even the smallest flinch would send Tommy scuttling away.

He crushed the bits of stick beneath his heel. "I know I act up sometimes . . . but my stepmom . . . she doesn't always act like she should."

"Does she hurt you?" I asked.

He did a move that was like a shrug and a nod at the same time.

I breathed in sharp. "Does your daddy know?"

"No," Tommy said. "And I don't want him to. He's already busy with his truck routes. He's gone a lot, and I know he hates it. I don't want to make things harder for him."

"You have to tell him," I urged him. "You have to, Tommy."

"No. I won't rat her out. It wouldn't be good for my brothers, either. I'm the only one she rags on. Anyway, you have to promise not to tell. You have to keep my secret like I'm keeping yours."

"I promise you, Tommy, but..." I thought about Momma's magical "please" back in New Orleans, and all the punch that one little word packed. "Words can be powerful. You should use yours to tell an adult if something bad is happening at home. Like Mrs. Boggs. She could help."

He scoffed. "Yeah, right. *My* words aren't powerful. You know what's really powerful? The words of an adult. Especially when they're being used to call you a liar."

"But—"

"Don't worry about me, May. Honest. I'm strong enough to handle it." Tommy grinned and banged his chest like a gorilla.

"You shouldn't have to be," I said quietly, but he pretended not to hear me.

· ✳ ·⁺ ✳ ·

In the morning, Mrs. Boggs triple-checked with me to make sure I still wanted to go back to Davenport.

I did.

After breakfast, we got on the highway, going in the opposite direction from Nashville. I sat with Pickle in my lap and watched the world blur by. There was a level of unreality to it, like I was watching a movie. Hadn't we just come this way? Was the world on rewind? But once I saw signs for Memphis, it became real.

The contest was happening the next day, and I wasn't going.

Even though I had never been to Nashville, when I closed my eyes, I could imagine it. The contest was happening at a place called the Walk of Fame Park. Maybe there would even be a velvety red carpet laid out for us to walk down. Karleen, the lady I'd spoken to on the phone, had told me that the contestants were supposed to gather at five p.m., an hour before the show. Then the judges and the crowd would arrive. My daddy would be there, sitting at the judges' table, smiling sunbeams at everyone who came onto that stage.

Except not at me. Not anymore.

It was okay, though. I was fine. I had made my decision, and that was that. Plus, it had been so long since I'd heard my daddy's radio show, I was excited to get back to Louisiana, where I could listen in without Mrs. Boggs breathing down my neck. I told myself being able to listen to him four days a week was as good as meeting him in person.

I almost believed it, too.

We spent the night parked on a side street in a quiet neighborhood on the outskirts of Memphis. Mrs. Boggs wasn't in the mood to pay for an RV campground again, and I didn't blame her. Thankfully, neither Tommy or Mrs. Boggs said much to me during dinner. In fact, I think one of the only things that was said was when Mrs. Boggs announced, "Now that we've got the time, I'd like to stop at that pop-up modern art museum I read about the other day. I kept the magazine article, which is around here somewhere. I think it's pretty close to here."

"I'll wait in the RV with Pickle," Tommy said quickly.

"No, you won't. You're both coming in with me. That dog will survive a few hours by himself."

"That's not fair! May got to stay with him while we were at Graceland."

"You're coming. And that's final."

"Aww," Tommy moaned. "But it's going to be so boring!"

"Oh, shush. It will be good for you."

Later that night, when I took Pickle out to do his business, something strange happened. A couple walked toward us on the sidewalk, and as they got closer, Pickle lost his mind. He started barking and straining and baring his tiny teeth as if he intended to chase them down and chew on their ankles. He lunged and tugged at the end of his leash as they passed.

"Control your dog," the woman said.

"Sorry, ma'am. Sir. I'm so sorry." I scooped Pickle into my arms, wheelchair and all. He was shaking worse than ever. He kept barking and growling at them and baring his teeth. "Stop that, Pickle! What's wrong with you?"

The coupled walked off. The woman had short brown hair, but the man—the man had a shiny bald head. Just like the man from the hot dog restaurant, Pickle's awful ex-owner.

Right away I felt bad for yelling at Pickle. Because he wasn't being difficult—he was afraid.

I made shushing sounds and rocked him back and forth in my arms. He only started to calm down once the man and woman turned the corner and disappeared from sight.

"Don't worry, Pickle," I said. "Try to breathe. It will all be okay. Trust me. I'm not going anywhere."

CHAPTER 24

There was a furious thunderstorm later that night. Even though Mrs. Boggs's RV was about as heavy as a bus, it rocked back and forth in the wind, and the rain pummeled the sides like someone was sloshing buckets of water against the windows. I imagined it was the same kind of storm that sent Noah packing all of his animals up into his ark.

But somehow, when Mrs. Boggs woke us up the next morning, the storm was gone, and in its place was cheery sunshine. Mrs. Boggs was up and out of bed earlier than her usual wake-up time.

"Rise and shine," she said, clapping her hands together. "I want to get to the museum early, before the lines. Come on, you lazy bums. Up, up, up!"

My eyes were closed, but I could hear Tommy

groaning into his pillow. "There won't be a line. No one is going to want to go to a stupid museum in the middle of nowhere."

"We're not in the middle of nowhere. We're in the suburbs of Memphis."

As we ate breakfast, Mrs. Boggs warned us not to get too filled up. "I heard they have delicious split pea soup at the museum café. Very green and not too lumpy."

Tommy widened his eyes in disgust and then started shoveling in his scrambled eggs twice as quickly.

After we finished, Mrs. Boggs instructed us to get Pickle ready for a walk while she called the museum to make sure they were still open, on account of the rain.

Tommy stared at her. "Why wouldn't it be open? Aren't museums inside?"

"Watch that lip, young man."

Turns out it *was* open, so after Pickle had done his business, Mrs. Boggs started driving us toward the museum.

"How long do we have to stay for?" Tommy asked.

"Oh, I don't know," Mrs. Boggs replied. "Four, maybe five hours."

"Great," Tommy grumbled, slumping down in his seat.

Ten minutes later, we pulled into a wide parking lot. I heard music. Carnival-style music. And that's when the Ferris wheel came into view.

"Wait a second," Tommy said, jumping to his feet. "This isn't an art museum! It's a fair!"

The RV lurched to a stop, and Mrs. Boggs spun around, a Cheshire cat's smile on her face. "Surprise! You ready to go on some rides?"

"No way! Are you serious?" Tommy shouted. "I've never been to a fair before!"

I thought nothing would be able to shake me from my fog, but even I felt a jolt of excitement. Now I understood why Mrs. Boggs had to call about the weather. I had been to a fair with Momma years ago, back when we lived in Baton Rouge. We ate cotton candy that stained our tongues blue and rode the spinning teacups so many times that our stomachs hurt from laughing so hard.

This was exactly what I needed, and somehow Mrs. Boggs knew it.

There were a bunch of families with kids around our age already waiting to buy their tickets. We joined the long line behind a pale, twitchy boy a little younger than Tommy and me, who was standing with his parents. The boy let out a high-pitched shriek when a car's engine misfired in the parking lot behind us. Tommy quit his excited squirming and bouncing long enough to laugh at him, which Mrs. Boggs cut short with one quick glare.

There were puddles everywhere from the storm the night before, but the sky was now a brilliant blue and the air had cooled down a few degrees. It was a perfect day for an outdoor concert in Nashville.

As we waited, I did the math in my head. There were seven hours until all the contestants were due to gather. Maybe they'd chitchat, maybe there would be a snack table with pie and pitchers of lemonade. Eight hours until the contest would begin. Would there be a curtain and a stage? Would the judges mingle and get to know the contestants beforehand?

I felt the squeeze of Mrs. Boggs's hand on my shoulder. "May? I said, here's your ticket."

"What? Oh. Thanks." Somehow we had gotten to the front of the line without my noticing. I took my ticket and followed her in, sidestepping muddy bits of ground.

"Wow!" Tommy shouted, running ahead of us. "Look at all these games! Ring toss and water guns! And look— that stall has cotton candy! Oh, and funnel cakes and candy apples! Look at that one with chocolate and peanut butter and crushed Oreos! Dang. I wish I hadn't eaten so much breakfast."

Mrs. Boggs chuckled. "I warned you not to fill up. Though it's probably best if you avoid all that junk."

"Oh, I'm still going to eat everything," Tommy said, patting his stomach. "I think I'll start with a funnel cake."

He reached into his pockets and pulled out a couple crumpled dollar bills from his lottery win, but Mrs. Boggs took out a bunch of cherry-colored tickets from her purse and handed half to me and half to Tommy. "Your money isn't any good here. The tickets are for games, snacks, and rides. Have fun, you two."

Tommy and I each took our handful of tickets, thanking Mrs. Boggs again and again.

Over the next hour, Tommy and I rode the Ferris wheel, the teacups (he spun our cup around even faster than Momma did), and the swings. I brought my tape recorder up with me to record the whoosh of air, the *ding-dong* music, and the happy screams of kids riding the swings with us. It came out pretty good. Tommy and I also tossed rings onto soda bottles (or *tried* to, at least) and shot targets with water guns. I had my eye on a duck stuffed animal I wanted to get for Pickle, so I played the water gun game again and again until I finally won it. Tommy spent a bunch of his tickets on snacks, and by the time he finished the last of his cotton candy, his face was a little green.

"Whoa. Would you look at that one," Mrs. Boggs said.

She was pointing at a ride that looked like it went up around two hundred feet into the air. I had to squint to see that there were people strapped into seats up there, their legs dangling.

A huge blinking sign announced the ride was called the Brain Shaker. I only had to wonder for a few seconds why it was called that, because suddenly the bottom of the ride fell out. It spun around and upside down, and with it came the sounds of screaming. It didn't sound like happy screaming, either. In that moment I was grateful my feet were planted firmly on the wonderful, beautiful pavement.

"That one looks fun," Mrs. Boggs said. "I like scary rides."

Tommy clutched his stomach and turned even greener. "I don't think I would feel so good after that."

Mrs. Boggs turned to me. "May? You want to ride it with me?"

I definitely did not. Especially so soon after one of my attacks, I didn't want to risk putting myself into a situation in which it might happen again. The idea of falling and spinning upside down and shaking while having a panic attack was enough to set my heart pounding. "I don't think so, ma'am. Sorry."

"Well, all right. We should get back on the road, so let's meet back at the RV in, let's say . . . fifteen minutes."

Tommy said he needed to sit down and rest his stomach, so he was going back to the RV early. I wasn't quite ready to go yet. I still had a few tickets, so I went exploring to see what I should use them on.

I was walking by a balloon dart game when I caught sight of the nervous boy I'd seen in line. His mother was nowhere to be seen, but his daddy was crouched down and pointing at one of the balloons, talking to the boy in a low voice. Then he must have said something funny, because the boy laughed. I couldn't help but wonder what he said.

The boy bit his tongue, closed one eye, and shot the dart. He missed by about five feet. It was a terrible shot, but his dad cheered for him anyway. "Great improvement, sport! Way closer than the last ones. You want to try again?"

The boy shook his head. "Can we go on a ride?"

"Sure. Let's look around."

I don't know why, but I followed them. Maybe I wanted to see what ride they chose. Or maybe I just wanted to be around someone's daddy, even if he wasn't my own.

The boy shook his head at the bumper cars, the swings, the teacups, and the haunted house. Following them felt like picking at a scab—good and painful at the same time. Finally, they came upon the Brain Shaker, right as the bottom dropped out and the screams started. I waited for the boy to have the same reaction to it as I did. Maybe he'd drop down in a dead faint or lose what little color he had in his pale face. From what I could see, he seemed like the kind of boy who would be scared out of his skin if so much as a fly was to land on his picnic plate.

But that's not what happened at all.

"This one," the boy said. He stepped up to the ticket taker without a second's hesitation. His daddy was the one to follow *him,* not the other way around.

As the riders filed off, visibly shaken, I watched the scaredy-cat boy jump up and down with excitement as he and his daddy waited to be allowed on. I couldn't believe it. How could a boy that twitchy be less afraid of something than me? It didn't make any sense.

Before the ride operator took their tickets, the daddy put a hand on his son's shoulder and said, "Hold on, Miles."

Then he turned around and looked directly at me.

"Hey, sweetheart. I've noticed you've been standing there watching the ride for a while. Are you out of tickets?" He dug around in his pocket. "We've got a few extras, if you want them. You can ride with us."

"*Dad,*" the boy said.

"We can always buy some more, son." Then he looked back at me and smiled. "So? What do you say?"

I was so taken aback that he'd noticed me, I could only mutter, "No. No, thank you. I've got my own tickets."

"All right, then." He turned back to the ride operator and handed over two tickets, one for his son and one for him.

I watched them get strapped in and ready to go. They

looked so happy. How bad could it be, really? At that moment, a quiet voice from deep inside me rose up.

It's not too late, it told me. *It's not too late to be brave.*

Only, the voice wasn't coming from anywhere in my head. It was coming from my heart.

"Wait!" I shouted. I grabbed a ticket from my pocket and rushed up to the ride before I could stop myself. The operator was about to close the gate, but he let me on.

I went up to where the man was sitting with his son and slid into the seat next to them. Once I'd had my seat restraints checked, the boy's daddy nodded at me. "Changed your mind, I see. I'm impressed."

"Thank you," I tried to say, but the ride's frantic music stole my words away. The ride started to ratchet up, up, and up into the sky. I squeezed my eyes shut, praying that my seat belt wasn't broken.

When we jolted to a stop, I forced myself to crack one eye open. I gasped. We were at the top. I could see all the way to rolling green pastures, with tiny white specks that must have been cows. I wondered if I could see all the way to Nashville from here. We were so high up, and now there was nowhere to go but down.

And that's when the bottom dropped out.

All the wind was knocked from my lungs, and it felt like my brain was rattling around in my head like a marble in a tin can. My stomach lifted and dropped; the world spun and stretched and went blurry. Someone was screaming like a steaming teakettle, and it took me a bunch of long, stretched-out seconds to realize that person was me.

And then it slowed. And stopped. And then it was like everything was slowed down to the speed of molasses, like I was in a dream as the ride operator started helping us all out of our seats. And just like that, I was on solid ground again.

"That was awesome!" the twitchy boy said to his daddy. "Can we ride it again?"

I waved shyly at them before I slipped away into the crowd.

I knew I wouldn't ride the Brain Shaker again, not ever, not if you paid me a million dollars, but even so, I was exhilarated. I had done it. I had done something I was afraid of, and here I was, still standing on two legs. Alive. And that was just the power I got from being near *someone else's* daddy.

Imagine what I could do if my real daddy was around to help me?

I could do anything.

That's when I knew exactly what I had to do. What I *could* do. I had to try. Even if I messed it all up, it was worth taking the chance. I calculated the hours in my head. I still had time.

I raced out of the park, past the EXIT ONLY sign hanging

on the fence, into the parking lot. I ran to the RV and banged in through the door.

Mrs. Boggs was reading a book in the driver's seat, with Pickle in her lap. She looked up in alarm when she saw me. "May? Is everything o—"

"We need to turn this RV around!" I cried. "We have to go back to Nashville. I can do it! I can sing!"

CHAPTER 25

Mrs. Boggs didn't hesitate for a second. "First things first, we've got to get some fuel, both for me and this gal," she said, thumping her free hand against the steering wheel. "So, both of you take a seat, and someone take Pickle!"

We screeched out of the parking lot, our tires leaving clouds of dust rising up behind us. People in line for the fair turned to stare. I waved at them from my seat, up front with Mrs. Boggs, Pickle in my lap. I felt breathless with a mixture of excitement and fear. I was still terrified, of course. But for the first time, I knew I could do it.

For the first time, I believed in myself.

"You know, May," Mrs. Boggs said, not taking her eyes off the road. "I think you're making the right decision."

"Me too!" Tommy called out from the couch. He was grinning from ear to ear, his Elvis sideburns now just dirty smudges on the sides of his face. "Definitely me too!"

When we stopped for gas, Mrs. Boggs gave Tommy a handful of bills and instructed him to run inside and get her two extra-large energy drinks. He looked shocked. "Really? *You're* gonna drink them? Even *I* know those things are filled with chemicals."

"By my calculations, we only have a little over five hours to make it there on time, so we can't stop for more than a few minutes. Desperate times, desperate measures. Now go!"

Five hours had never felt so long and also so short as on the way to Nashville. It was as if the blood running through my veins was electrified. For the first four hours, I couldn't sit still. I fidgeted and shook my legs and stretched my jaw and tugged on my ponytail. I wished I could tell Mrs. Boggs to step on it, drive faster, but I knew she was pushing herself as it was. Every time the cars in front of us slowed down even the tiniest bit, I leaned forward and stared at the traffic with such intensity, Mrs. Boggs finally had to tell me to knock it off because I was making her nervous.

The only time I felt like I could relax was when I had Pickle snoozing in my lap. Mrs. Boggs was the one who pointed it out. "Maybe you should bring Pickle up onstage when it's your turn to sing," she suggested. "That dog brings out the calm inside you."

"Oh! You think they'd let me?" I hugged Pickle a little closer.

"I don't see why not. People bring their dogs with them everywhere these days. It's worth a try."

I kissed the top of Pickle's head, and as I did, I noticed there were little pieces of something pink around his snout—like pieces of shredded pink paper. Hopefully he hadn't been chewing on one of Mrs. Boggs's books while we were at the fair. And if he had been, I hoped it wasn't an important one. I really had to teach him to stop chewing on things. I brushed the paper off his nose quickly so Mrs. Boggs wouldn't notice.

It must have stormed across Tennessee the night before, too, because there were huge puddles all over the highway we had to spray through, like we were adventurers slogging through the jungle.

"Wow!" cried Mrs. Boggs, draining the last of her energy drink. She crushed the can and threw it over her shoulder. "These things may be cancer in a can, but phew, do they work!"

"Can I have one?" Tommy asked. "Please?"

"Absolutely not. I'd have to get a broom to peel you off the ceiling."

"Awww," he moaned.

Once we were within a half hour of Nashville, I realized we were going to make it by five. And if Mrs. Boggs kept up her pace, we'd actually have time to spare.

It was right about then that Pickle started squirming

in my lap and howling. I tried to quiet him down, but it wasn't joyful howling. It was the *I have to go number two* kind of howling.

Mrs. Boggs looked over at us. "That dog has to go to the bathroom. And so do I, come to think of it. Those drinks went right through me. I'll pull off at the next rest area. It should be coming up soon."

Pickle nearly wriggled right on out of my lap once Mrs. Boggs pulled the RV to a stop at the rest area off Mile 169.

Once we parked, Mrs. Boggs tilted her head side to side, cracking her neck. Then she checked her watch. "I want to be safe, so we can't spend more than ten minutes here. May, why don't you use this time to put on that beautiful dress of yours?"

Of course—my dress! I'd kept the box stashed in Mrs. Boggs's bedroom, so I'd almost forgotten about it.

Mrs. Boggs was hurrying to the bathroom as she spoke. "And, Tommy, take Pickle out to do his business. Let him run around and burn off some energy. Best he be tired out and calm if he's going to be up onstage with May."

"I'm on it!" Tommy replied, grabbing Pickle's wheelchair. I handed Pickle off to him and made my way back toward Mrs. Boggs's room to change. The excitement wasn't just inside me—it must have been thrumming in the air, because both Mrs. Boggs and Tommy had clearly been breathing it in.

I hadn't touched the box with my dress since the lady packed it up for me at the department store back in Jackson. I hoped the dress had the same magic now as it did in the store.

But when I went back into Mrs. Boggs's bedroom, to the corner of the room where I'd stashed it, I found it wasn't a box anymore.

It was a pile of chewed-up pieces.

"No!" I cried.

I fell to my knees to sort through the wreckage, but the damage had been done. The skirt of my dress was nothing but shreds of silver, with wet pieces of pink tissue paper dotting it like sad confetti. Of all the things to chew in this RV—of all the boxes—why did Pickle have to choose *this* one? Tears pricked my eyes. I was glad Pickle wasn't back there with me right then, because, oh, how I wanted to shout at him. To yell, *Bad dog!* And in that moment, I wouldn't have even cared if he shook and trembled. Because he'd done a terrible thing. All that money, wasted. I couldn't even return it now.

Forcing myself to get up, I grabbed my bag and dumped it out on the foot of Mrs. Boggs's bed. I rustled through it. Raggedy tank tops, sundresses, jean shorts. Nothing compared at all to my starlight dress.

There was a knock at the door. "May? Everything okay in there? I heard a shout."

"My dress." My voice warbled. "Pickle ruined it."

Mrs. Boggs pushed open the door and lifted her hand to her mouth when she saw the damage. "Oh no. What else do you have to wear?"

I pointed at my sad lump of worn-out clothes on the foot of her bed. "Not much."

She sorted through it, shaking her head. "No. None of this will do." Then the look on her face changed. "Hold on. I've got an idea."

Mrs. Boggs threw open her closet door and pushed aside the clothes on the hangers. From the far back, she pulled out a box, opened its top, and tipped its contents out on the bed next to my clothes.

I gasped. It was a riot of colors. A rainbow of dresses, pants, and shirts. "These look like the clothes you were wearing in your old photo album."

"They are. Some of them, at least," Mrs. Boggs said. She was looking through the pile, all business.

I went over to touch a soft, bluish purple dress. Periwinkle. That was the name of the color. "I thought you got rid of them."

"No. And it's a good thing I didn't," Mrs. Boggs said, holding the periwinkle dress up against me. "Because this one is perfect for you. I'll just need to pin it up in a few places. Put it on and I'll go get some safety pins from the front."

I did as I was told. The color was pretty, but the dress itself slumped around me, with straps that were far too long for my shoulders. I could only hope Mrs. Boggs knew what she was doing.

She came back in with a determined look on her face, safety pins in her mouth. She knelt down next to me. "Don't move. I don't want to stick you."

I stilled my body as best I could as she got to work. Doing something nice for me. Again. "Thank you," I told her. "Thank you for everything you've done for me. I'll find a way to make it all up to you. I promise."

Her fingers stopped moving. "I already told you," she said firmly. "I don't mind it. Just try to remember how good you feel taking care of Pickle. That's how I feel taking care of you. Let me."

I sighed. I knew she was right, but it was one thing to take care of someone and it was something else entirely to let someone take care of you. "Okay. I know. But still. I want to make it up to you."

Her fingers got to work again, tugging and pinning. "May, you already have."

"What do you mean? I haven't done anything."

There was a long pause.

"Remember when you asked why I was willing to watch you for so long?"

"Yeah. You said it was the right thing to do."

"Yes. And that was true. Your mother is a good woman who needed help. But somewhere along the way, it went from being 'the right thing' to 'the best thing.' For me, I mean. You know, I haven't been to a fair in years. I haven't laughed so much or slept so well since Darryl . . . since Darryl died." Her voice caught, and she cleared her throat. "These past few days have felt almost . . . magical." She laughed a little. "Minus all the traffic."

I smiled. "I thought you said you didn't believe in magic."

"Well, maybe things can change. Now stop wiggling or I really am going to poke you with this pin."

I kept smiling, and did as she told me to.

A few minutes later, she sat back on her knees. "There. All done."

I looked in the mirror. The dress was lumpy and a tiny bit uneven in a few places, but it actually fit me now. I looked like me. In fact, when I squinted my eyes a little, it even looked *pretty*. I still wished I was going up onstage in my beautiful silver dress, presenting a perfect version of myself. But maybe, at the end of the day, it was better to be honest about who I was. Lumpy fabric and all.

As I swung back and forth, looking at myself from different angles, Mrs. Boggs went to sweep all those colorful clothes back into the box they'd been in.

"Wait," I said. "Don't put them at the back of the closet again. Maybe you can hang some of them up."

"You know," Mrs. Boggs said, after staring at the pile for a while. She smiled. "Maybe I will." She checked the clock on her nightstand. "Later, though. We've got to get back on the road."

· ✳ · + ✳ ·

As we exited the highway onto Broadway, a street in downtown Nashville, I was so amazed by our surroundings, I almost forgot to be nervous.

"Welcome to Music City," Mrs. Boggs said.

I craned my neck as we passed a building that looked like an old stone castle straight out of a fairy tale.

"That's Union Station," she said. "Used to be a train station, and now it's a fancy hotel. I forgot how much I loved this city."

And that wasn't all. We passed more old-fashioned buildings made of both brick and weathered stone. Beyond the tidy sidewalks were pretty green parks and tiny gardens filled with colorful flowers. Broadway was a big, six-lane street, and I don't think I saw a single piece of litter anywhere on the pavement.

"We're not in Davenport anymore, Toto," I whispered to Pickle as we turned onto Sixth Avenue. I was still sad about what he'd done to my dress. I'd even started to scold him when Tommy first brought him back inside at the rest area. But one look at his big brown eyes made any anger I had left inside me evaporate like steam. He was only a dog, after all, with a past filled with too much anger already. For Pickle's sake, I would teach him not to chew on my precious things, without any shouting or yelling. That, and I'd keep all my things up on a counter-top where he couldn't reach them.

We were about to turn left onto Demonbreun Street when we hit a monster traffic snarl. I opened my window and stuck my head out to see how bad it was. There was a snaking line of cars and police lights flashing up ahead.

"Hmm. The street must be blocked off." Mrs. Boggs motioned at the huge building to our right. The entire front wall was made of glimmering glass windows and skinny brown columns. "I think that's the Music City Center. There must be a convention happening. Maybe I can turn around."

Mrs. Boggs shifted into reverse, and the rearview camera popped up. "Shoot. There are cars already piled up behind me."

She was right—we were completely boxed in.

"Nooo," I moaned. Not when we were so close! A few weeks ago it felt like the universe was shining down a light to guide me to Nashville. Now it felt like it was doing everything it could to keep me from getting there.

"But, May," Mrs. Boggs said, "we aren't far. All you

have to do is hop out and walk three long blocks that way, and the Walk of Fame Park will be right there on your left. Got it?"

Three blocks? I could walk three blocks with my eyes closed! I scrambled to gather up my belongings. I grabbed my cell phone, just in case. Pickle's wheelchair was a little muddy from the rest station, so I shoved it in a plastic shopping bag before gathering Pickle up in my arms.

Mrs. Boggs grasped my hand. "Go, May. This snarl can't last for too long. We'll be there in time to see the show no matter what, so don't you worry. You can do this. I believe in you."

"I believe in you, too, May," Tommy said from behind me. When I turned, he was waiting, his hand on the RV door. "Now let's go!"

Mrs. Boggs stared at him. "Nuh-uh. No. You're staying with me, Mr. O'Brien."

"You'll either have to tie me up or put rocks in my shoes to keep me from going with her, Mrs. Boggs," Tommy said cheerfully. "Sorry."

Mrs. Boggs sighed deeply and then muttered something under her breath. "Fine, then. Go. But the two of you stay together, you understand? Don't go exploring the park on your own."

"I won't," Tommy promised, grinning. "And we will."

I blew Mrs. Boggs a kiss before Tommy and I hopped

down from the RV onto the pavement. As I did, I felt a tickle in my throat. The words to Momma's song were already starting to bubble up inside me like they were going to lift me up off my feet, they were so ready to come out. Because it wasn't only Mrs. Boggs and Tommy who believed in me—*I* finally did, too. I knew I shouldn't burst into song there on the sidewalk, so I did my best to tamp them back down.

But it didn't *quite* work. Because even though the handles of the plastic bag were digging into the crook of my elbow and I had Pickle's warm weight gathered up in my arms, I didn't just run down the sidewalk.

I flew.

CHAPTER 26

As soon as we reached the Walk of Fame Park, I stopped short.

Something wasn't right.

The park wasn't nearly as big as I'd imagined. This was just a normal city park, surrounded by a bunch of tall steel-and-glass buildings. But that wasn't the problem.

The problem was the crowd. The park was already filled with people, sitting, standing, bopping their heads to the music filling the air around us. Music. Why was there already music? We were across the street from the park, looking at the back of the stage, so I couldn't see, but I could definitely hear that there was a woman up there, singing into a microphone and strumming her guitar.

It didn't make any sense. Had they started the contest

early for some reason? Or maybe it was some kind of a practice session? What was going on?

"Wow," Tommy said, joining me. He put his hands on his knees and tried to catch his breath. "You're fast. You should join the track team at school." A second later, he seemed to notice the crowd and the singer already onstage. "Um, May? Are you, uh, sure you got the time right?"

As soon as he said it, I knew. It hit me like someone had tipped a bucket of ice down the back of my dress.

The contest wasn't early—*I* was late.

An *hour* late.

Somewhere along the way, I'd messed it up. I'd mis-remembered the time.

I wasn't supposed to *be there* at five.

The contest *started* at five.

Which meant . . . my daddy was already there. I couldn't see the judges' table from back where I was, but surely he was there.

"I got it wrong," I said. "How could I have been so stupid? Why didn't I write it down?"

"Well, there's no use in just standing here. What's done is done. I bet there's still time. And look," Tommy said. "Over there." He was pointing at a white tent, to the right of the stage. A set of rough wooden steps led up to a doorway flap with a sign on it that said PRIVATE.

"I bet that's where you're supposed to be. Come on. Let's go."

Tommy checked traffic both ways and then started jogging across the street. I hitched Pickle under my arm and followed him, my heart beating wildly.

Please don't let it be too late, I thought. *Please, please, please.*

We'd only just gone up the stairs when a pretty woman with huge blond hair and a clipboard tucked beneath her arm stepped out from behind the tent's opening, stopping us from going any farther.

"Uh-uh-uh," she said. "You can access the audience area from the other sidewalk. This area's private. For contestants only."

I froze. "I—I—"

"She *is* a contestant," Tommy said, giving me a little shove forward.

"Yes," I said, swallowing. "He's right. I am. I'm sorry I'm late, but I'm here. My name is Maybelle Lane."

The song being performed came to an end, followed by thunderous applause.

A voice rang out of the loudspeakers. "Let's all put it together for Sasha Mae Franklin, here from Knoxville, Tennessee! And now, for our next contestant. . . ."

The lady looked at the clipboard. "It does appear we're missing one, but you were supposed to be here by four.

The contest's already begun. I'm sorry, sweet pea. You're too late."

"You have to let me on," I begged, wiping sweat from my brow with my arm. "You have no idea what it took for me to get here."

"You're over an hour late. You brought a friend. *And you brought your dog*," she said, eyeing Pickle. "Which is so completely inappropriate, I don't even know where to start. Now tell me why in the Lord's name should I let you on that stage?"

Why should she let me on that stage? I stood taller, hitching Pickle higher under my arm. I imagined myself strong and commanding, like Mrs. Boggs had been back in the hotel hallway when she'd made that red-faced man apologize to me. I took a deep breath, filling my words with as much strength and power as I could muster. "I'll tell you why. It took me a week of driving in an RV to get here. I'm terrified of singing onstage, I think it might be my worst fear in the whole world, but I'm going to do it anyway. And you know why?" I pointed out to the crowd. "Because one of those men out there in the crowd is my daddy. We've never met, but I'm going to sing my song with everything I've got and win his heart."

"Woo!" Tommy said, punching the air. "You tell her, May!"

The lady's eyes had gone wide at my words. Then

they sort of went . . . fluttery. I could only hope that was a good sign. Then she pressed her hand to her chest. "Well, if that isn't the sweetest thing I've ever heard in my whole entire life. I'll tell you what," she said. "I'll let you go on, but it has to be our little secret. But your dog can't come."

"No," I said, hugging Pickle closer. "I need him. His name's Pickle. He's a good boy, I promise you."

Mostly good boy, I thought, picturing my shredded-up dress.

She shook her head. "I'm sorry, but no. The rules are the rules."

"He's her emotional support animal, ma'am," Tommy said smoothly. "Right, May?"

I had no idea where Tommy pulled that idea from, but I could tell he wanted me to go along with it. "Oh, yes," I said. "Yes, that's right."

"He helps with her anxiety, see," Tommy added. "His official papers are back at home. Wouldn't it be terrible if *you* were the one who told her she couldn't bring him up with her and then something bad happened?"

"Hmm," she said, after a long pause. "Well, all right. I see your point. I suppose you can bring him."

"Thank you!" I cried. "Oh, thank you, ma'am!"

"Now all I need is for you to go get a parent or a legal guardian to sign the release forms. Since you're under the age of sixteen."

The forms.

I'd completely forgotten that I had to have an adult fill out forms for me. I had told myself I'd cross that bridge when I came to it, and here I was, at the bridge—with absolutely no plan at all.

She smiled big and wide at me with her bright white Chiclet teeth. "Okay?"

Tommy scuffed the ground with his shoe and didn't say anything.

Think, Maybelle.

"My momma is, uh, stuck in traffic. That's why I'm all sweaty. I ran here. She'll sign them after the show."

She let out a sigh. "You better be telling me the truth. I'll be here waiting after the show with these for your mother to fill out. If you're fibbing, I could get fired, and I love this job. I'll make sure you'll be in a world of trouble. You hear me?"

At the very worst, I'd ask my daddy to sign them. He was a parent, right? "Hi, I'm your daughter, now sign these forms" wasn't the best way to introduce myself, but at least it would mean no one would get fired. "Yes. Yes, ma'am."

"Good." She fluffed her hair, apparently satisfied with my answer. "And I'm much too young to be a ma'am, don't you think? My name's Miss Georgia Lord: Georgia like the peaches, Lord like Jesus. You can call me Miss Lord. I'm the event coordinator."

"How long before it's May's turn?" Tommy asked.

"I'll have her go last. So . . ." She tapped her lips with a perfectly manicured finger. "Maybe thirty minutes? Thirty-five?"

Thirty minutes? That wasn't a lot of time.

"Got it." Tommy turned to me. "I'm going to run back to the RV and tell Mrs. Boggs we have to hurry. I bet she's barely moved. We won't miss your song," he said, grabbing my hands. "I promise. Break a leg, May. Actually, no," he added, grinning. "Break 'em both."

Miss Lord tittered. "Well. Let's hope it doesn't come to that. Now thank your lucky stars I'm in such a friendly mood, and come on in before any more time is wasted."

I said goodbye to Tommy, and then Miss Lord led me over to a plastic folding table that was covered with sweating pitchers of iced tea and half-eaten trays of cookies and little sandwiches that were already going stale around the corners. She grabbed a box below the table and opened it. "Here's your name tag."

She handed it to me. In big, bold letters, it said MAVEN LANE.

I stared at it. "Um . . ."

"Is something wrong?" she asked.

I'd already required such special treatment, I wasn't about to tell her that they'd gotten my name wrong. "No. Nothing."

"Good. If you want, you can get a peek through that

curtain to watch the show. Come get me if you need anything else."

"I will. Thank you, Miss Lord. Truly."

Miss Lord marched off to the other side of the tent to do whatever it is event coordinators do, leaving me and Pickle alone.

I didn't have any time to warm up.

I didn't have any time to relax.

But I was here, and that's what mattered.

Another contestant had gone up on the stage by then.

After I set Pickle down and got him rigged up in his wheelchair, I went over to the gap in the curtains Miss Lord had pointed to.

The stage was small, barely five feet off the ground. All sorts of colored lights were hanging from the top of it, even though the sun was still in the sky. A banner at the back of the stage showed a big logo for Bobby's Flamin' Hot Chicken, the restaurant sponsoring all the prizes. There were also a few tall clear vases arranged around the stage with something reddish orange inside them.

Hot sauce, I realized. The vases were full of hot sauce.

A low metal fence had been set up to separate the audience from the stage. Right between the fence and the stage was a table with a red-and-white-checkered tablecloth with four people sitting at it.

And one of them was my daddy.

I'm not sure I took a breath for a good two minutes as I watched him sitting there, bopping a pen against the table to the beat of the song being sung.

He was wearing a long-sleeve button-down shirt and a worn-in cowboy hat. He looked exactly like his picture, except he looked smaller somehow. Shorter, maybe. And when he took off his hat to wave it in the air when the singer finished, I noticed his hair was thinning at the top.

But these little realities didn't disappoint me. They only made me excited to get to know him better. Because here he was. In the flesh. A real person.

When I finally turned my attention to the other judges, my stomach seized.

Two of them were women judges, but the fourth judge was a man. He was enormous, towering over the others even when he was sitting, and he looked to be about three times wider than my daddy. But that's not what worried me.

What worried me was that he looked *exactly* like Pickle's old owner, only bigger. And scarier. His head was so bald it reflected the white light of the hot afternoon sun. I thought about how badly Pickle had reacted to that bald man on the sidewalk. He was terrified. Shaken down to his doggy core. How would he react to *this* man?

I chewed my lip, trying to decide what I should do about Pickle. Maybe Tommy was still here and he'd have an idea! I grabbed Pickle and raced to the tent's flap, but when I pushed it aside and looked around, he was nowhere to be seen. I even called his name, louder each time, but he never appeared.

Okay, so not Tommy. I could bring Pickle up and try to face him away from the crowd so he didn't notice the bald-headed judge. Or I could tie him up backstage and go on alone.

As I imagined that scenario, the edges of my vision went black and panic started rising in my throat. No. I needed him. Even though he didn't have any official papers, he really *was* my emotional support animal. I couldn't sing up there without him. And helping me out was the least he could do for chewing up my silver dress.

Or I could cover Pickle's eyes so he couldn't see anything at all! I ran over to the snack table and snatched a few napkins, as well as half a sandwich for myself, because all of a sudden I was starved. I tied the napkins together to make a sort of blindfold. He pawed it off right away. I put it on once more, and he did it again. That wouldn't work.

In fact, I had a feeling he was doing this so he could continue to stare at the sandwich that was in my hands. I took a piece of turkey out and wiggled it back and forth. Pickle never took his eyes off that piece of meat.

He licked his chops and focused on it with razor-sharp intensity.

That was it. I would hold a piece of turkey in my fist, to keep him from looking at the crowd.

It was going to work. It had to.

CHAPTER 27

As we waited for our turn, I kept peeking out at the crowd to watch my daddy. My daddy, and the way he never took his eyes off whoever was singing, the way he bopped his head to the beat, the way he obviously loved music and wanted to support the people brave enough to get up there and sing. But also because this was by far the biggest group I'd ever seen gathered in one place. Two, maybe three hundred people had to be out there, maybe more. The most people I had ever sung in front of was at my school's chorus show back in Baton Rouge, which was only about sixty or seventy people. A fraction of this.

The park seemed to stretch and transform back into the way I'd been imagining it on the way here: suddenly it felt larger than a football field, the crowd endless, the stage reaching into the heavens, lights flashing.

And every singer that went up was better than the last.

There was a woman with an Australian accent who sang a Rolling Stones song. Then came the Violets, a duo. They were full of soul and strumming, letting loose the kind of music that makes you feel like it was written only for you. They finished, and an old man called Buck Henderson, with a gray handlebar mustache, went up with a silver harmonica.

As the emcee announced him, someone tapped my shoulder. It was Miss Lord.

"Maven," she said, crossing something off on her clipboard. "You're up next. You ready?"

I patted my hair and smoothed my periwinkle dress. Strangely, I didn't feel nervous. My heart didn't race. I felt a cool and calm peacefulness inside me.

I nodded at Miss Lord. I was readier than I'd ever been in my life.

"Good. Then go stand over there, where the tape marks an X, and go out onstage when you get called."

I went to where I was told and watched Buck Henderson singing a sad song about a woman who didn't love him back. He played his instrument with the same care and tenderness Momma did. It nearly moved me to tears. As soon as he finished, he got a standing ovation from the judges. His was going to be a hard act to follow.

Then, before I knew what was happening, the emcee

had asked the crowd to put their hands together for "Maven Lane" and I was being waved onstage.

I swallowed. *It's now. Now, now, now . . .*

I went to the center of the stage and took the microphone from the emcee with my free hand. I glanced at the judges' table. One of the lady judges was staring at Pickle with a disapproving frown. Thankfully, the other three were all smiling and clapping, like seeing a wiener dog in a wheelchair onstage was nothing new to them.

My daddy's smile was the most encouraging one of all.

That's my daddy, I thought wildly. *That's my daddy looking at me.*

"Hello." I cleared my throat and leaned into the microphone. "My name's actually Mayb—" The word screeched through the speakers. People covered their ears. I gritted my teeth and breathed through my nose. I was messing it up already.

And that's when I heard someone from the audience shout, "You can do it, May!"

I knew that voice. I searched the crowd, shielding my eyes against the bright lights. Tommy! There, in the back, standing on a chair. Next to Tommy was Mrs. Boggs. They'd made it!

Seeing them restored me. I brought the microphone back up, but kept it farther away from my face. "I'll be singing an original song today, without musical accompaniment. It was written by my momma. I hope y'all enjoy."

There was another smattering of applause. I ignored the frenzied beating of my heart and began to sing.

"She came to me on a cold, dark night. . . ."

The first few lines came out of me like honey warmed by the sun. It felt right. *I* felt right. The crowd hushed up in a way they hadn't for the other singers. My daddy took off his hat and put it to his heart. I was doing it. I was singing!

I let myself get carried away by the song, like a dandelion puff on the breeze. I closed my eyes and gave myself over to it.

Which was a mistake. A big one. Because that's exactly when I must have accidentally dropped the turkey to the floor without noticing. Had my eyes been open, I could have bent down and picked it up before Pickle got to it. But that's not what happened.

After enjoying his treat, Pickle must have turned around. Maybe he squinted briefly against the bright lights. But then his vision must have cleared. And that's when he must have seen the judge with the big bald head.

Because he started yowling. And barking. And tugging on his leash. Someone in the crowd gasped as Pickle pulled on his leash so forcefully that it went flying out of my hand.

"Arr-ooo!" he howled. As soon as he was free, he started careening straight for the backstage area, but in his way was one of the big vases of hot sauce.

"Oh no!" I cried, chasing after him. I still had the microphone in my hand. The crowd was gasping by now. I lurched to grab the leash, but I was too late.

One of Pickle's wheels smashed into the vase of hot sauce. At first I hoped it was too heavy to be pushed over, but let me tell you, that little dog had some serious momentum. Because it tipped and teetered, back and forth, and then that vase of hot sauce came crashing down toward me and onto the stage with a loud *SMACK!*

The hot sauce went everywhere. And I didn't have enough time to slow down before I reached the puddle of it. So I slipped and went flying.

There were hundreds of people in the crowd that day, but in that moment it was so quiet you could have heard a pin drop. I lifted myself onto my elbows. At least Miss Lord had the good sense to grab Pickle's leash. She was trying to calm him down backstage.

That moment of silence was the loudest thing I'd ever heard. It couldn't really be happening.

Was I having a nightmare? The worst one of my life?

"Someone help this poor girl up!" the bald-headed judge finally called out. I glared at him. This whole thing was his fault. "Get her off the stage. Someone!"

I was about to get up and dash backstage when my daddy stood up. "Young lady," he said, his eyes full of kindness. He nodded encouragingly. "Would you like to finish your song?"

I swallowed shakily and shook my head no. Not now. Not anymore. Not ever again.

That's when I heard it. The warble of the guitar was far away at first, like I had imagined it drifting toward me on the breeze. But then it grew stronger. In the distance, I saw a woman standing on a folding chair at the back of the crowd. I couldn't make out her face, but the shape of her was familiar. And the chords coming out of her guitar—those were familiar, too.

They were the chords to Momma's song.

The woman standing there was Momma! She was standing so far away, she was almost just a silhouette. At first I thought I must have hit my head and she was a figment of my imagination—because wasn't she supposed to be in Miami?—but then she shouted, "Finish our song, May! I believe in you!"

I stood up. I wiped the hot sauce off me as best I could. I took a breath.

And with the chords from Momma's guitar floating in the air around me, I closed my eyes, dug deep down, and I finished our song.

CHAPTER 28

Everything that happened next was a blur.

One second I was singing, my fingers stinging and tingling from the fiery hot sauce, and the next second I was being ushered off the stage as the audience stamped, whistled, and hollered, "MAVEN, MAVEN, MAVEN . . ."

Most everyone was up on their feet. They hadn't exploded like that for any of the other contestants. Despite how disastrous my performance had been, it felt good to be clapped for like that.

I went directly for Pickle, who was shaking like he knew he'd messed something up. I scratched behind his ears and told him, "It's okay. Don't worry."

While I did my best to towel off some of the sticky hot sauce, the four judges scooted their chairs closer to the table and leaned their heads together, deep in discussion. After five minutes of conversing, they seemed to reach some sort of a decision, because they called us all back onto the stage.

The gray-haired lady judge whispered to Miss Lord, who got onto the stage and tapped a microphone. "Thanks again for coming out to our live radio contest today! We had some strong talent and some"—her eyes flicked to me—"exciting drama here today. We hope y'all will make it next year, for this is sure to be an annual event from here on out! Now, are you ready to hear who our winner is?"

The audience roared. So did the blood in my head, filling up my ears.

Miss Lord continued. "Please join me in applause for our winner, local Nashville resident Mr. Buck Henderson!"

He strolled over to Miss Lord, who was waiting with a big Styrofoam check. It was made out to BUCK HENDERSON, and instead of an amount of money, it was good for ONE YEAR'S WORTH OF BOBBY'S FLAMIN' HOT CHICKEN.

I was happy it was Buck. I was expecting to feel a tidal wave of disappointment as I watched the judges clap and the audience cheer for a winner who wasn't me, but I didn't. I already felt like I had gained something. I had lived my worst nightmare—I had made a fool of myself onstage in front of hundreds of people—but I had still sung my song.

That was who I was. Someone who didn't give up in the face of fear.

That was my story.

So I grinned and shouted and clapped louder for Mr. Buck Henderson than any of the other contestants onstage with me.

After we all went back to the private tented area, I knew my moment had arrived. I felt it sizzling in my bones. I was desperate to get a moment alone with my daddy before Momma and Mrs. Boggs and Tommy came rushing back to see me. Especially Momma. I could already see the crowd was starting to break apart, which meant I didn't have much time. Pickle was relaxing in the shade, and I didn't want to bring him with, so I chewed my lip until I saw Miss Lord sitting with Buck Henderson while he signed a bunch of winner's papers.

I went over to them.

Mr. Henderson smiled when he saw me. "Quite a performance, little lady. Voice like an angel. You should keep practicing."

"Thank you," I said, ducking my head. I could tell he meant it. Then I turned to Miss Lord. "Sorry, ma'am, but do you think you could watch my dog for a second? I'd like to go talk to one of the judges."

Miss Lord's eyes brightened. "Is it—is he . . ."

I nodded.

"You take as long as you need, sweet pea. I'll keep my eye on your dog. I'm rooting for you."

"Thank you."

I turned to go.

"And, darling? When you get back, I still need those forms!"

I made my way over to my daddy. He was talking to one of the women judges. She looked up when she saw me approaching.

"Well, hey there, Maven," she said. "Nice work onstage. Congratulations."

"Yes," my daddy agreed. "I wish all our radio shows had even a fraction of the excitement you gave us!"

I didn't say thank you. I didn't apologize for spilling hot sauce everywhere, and I didn't tell the lady my name was not Maven. I just stared straight at my daddy and asked, "Can I talk to you? Alone?"

The woman looked questioningly at my daddy.

He shrugged. "Well, sure, young lady, I don't see why not." He turned back to the woman. "I'll talk to you next week. You'll be on that conference call, won't you?"

"I will," she said. Then she shook my daddy's hand, and then mine, and went away.

It was just the two of us now. I scanned the crowd,

but I didn't see any signs of Momma or Mrs. Boggs or Tommy yet. Good. They had been at the far back of the crowd, so hopefully they'd be stuck there for at least a few more minutes. "Do you mind if we go talk over there?" I asked, pointing to a spot by the side of the stage. "It will be a little quieter that way."

And less chance we'll be found, I thought but did not add.

"Of course," he said.

We went along the side of the stage toward the back, almost to the sidewalk, with the Country Music Hall of Fame looming over us.

"Here good?" he asked.

"Perfect. I—"

"Wait one minute," he said. He reached into his pocket and pulled out a folded-up bandanna. "You've got a streak of hot sauce on your cheek. Here."

He handed me the bandanna, and I started rubbing my cheek at random. "Better?" I said.

"No, a little to the left—actually, do you mind if I just get it for you?"

I swallowed. "No. Not at all."

He bent down and carefully wiped my cheek. He didn't scrub hard or anything. I hardly felt it. "There. Much better."

When he smiled, I thought I might faint.

"You know, I'm glad you asked to talk to me," he said, tucking the bandanna back in his pocket.

"You are?"

He nodded. "I wanted to tell you that what you did up there was very impressive. Not only finishing your song after you fell . . . but also your singing. Have you ever had any voice training?"

"No," I told him.

He whistled. "Well, darn. Well then, let me just say you've got more talent in your pinky finger than most musicians I've ever met. With a little training and a lot of practice, I think you could be something sublime."

"You do?" I breathed.

"I do. So keep going. Never give up." He clapped his hands together. "Now, what is it you wanted to talk to me about?"

I gave him my most winning smile. "I'm a big fan. I listen to your show every day it's on."

If my performance had been a nightmare, this was a dream come true. *He* was a dream come true. I was talking to my daddy, and I wasn't even choking on any of my words.

"Thanks, sweetheart. It's so nice to be back in the South after living in Los Angeles for so long."

So *that's* why I'd never heard his show my whole life! He hadn't mentioned on his show that he'd lived out west. The first mystery, solved. And Los Angeles—wow! All I could think of were palm trees and Hollywood stars. I wanted to hear everything. There were so many things I still didn't know about him.

Then he cocked his head at me, a funny expression on his face. "By any chance, do we know each other? You seem familiar to me."

It was now.

It was my moment.

"No," I said. "Not yet. But we will. My name isn't Maven. It's Maybelle Dorothy Lane. And, well . . . I'm your daughter."

The color drained right out of his face, like it does in the cartoons. I imagined it pooling at his toes. He gaped at me. "Lane? As in Gemma Lane?"

He remembered her! "Yes. That's my momma."

"Oh my God. Oh my Lord. You look exactly like the baby pictures she used to send me. Oh my God. I need to sit down."

"Wait . . . what? Pictures?" I asked. "What pictures?"

"Your baby pictures," he repeated, a dazed look on his face.

But how would he have seen my baby pictures? That didn't make any sense.

Unless . . .

Unless Momma *had* told him about me.

I stared at him. "Do you . . . do you already know who I am?"

He ran his hand through his hair and then put his hat back on. "Well, yes. Yes."

"When . . ." The words weren't coming easily. "When did she send pictures to you?"

"I don't know. It was years ago. When you were a baby."

I couldn't believe it. Momma had lied to me. She *had* told my daddy I existed.

"You . . . you've known you had a daughter this whole time? But . . . but what about all those things you said on the radio?"

"What do you mean, on the radio?"

"When my friend Tommy called in and asked you that question. About having a baby you didn't know about."

A look of understanding flashed across his face. "*You* were behind that phone call the other day? Oh God, Maybelle." He shifted uncomfortably. "See . . . it's just . . . you can't believe everything you hear on the radio. I've got an image to uphold with my listeners. Technically, I'm a radio DJ, but some days it's more like I'm a talk therapist. My listeners need to trust me. Which means I've got to be as near perfect on air as humanly possible, but also relatable. Do you understand?"

No. I did not understand. By that point, my whole

body was shaking. "You've known about me for eleven years, and you've never called? You never wrote, you never visited?"

"I wasn't ready to be a father back then. I wasn't in a good place."

"So be a father now. I'm right here."

"It's not as simple as that. My wife has no idea. It would complicate things."

"So complicate them!"

"Please," he said, his eyes darting around. "Lower your voice. I have a family."

Those words hit me like a fist to the chest. But what hurt even more were the unspoken ones.

I have a family, Maybelle, and it doesn't include you.

"Rick?" A pretty blond lady with a huge pregnant belly, like someone had shoved a watermelon down her shirt, waddled toward us. "Rick, you coming, sweetheart? Who's that you're talking to?"

He stepped in front of me, hiding me from view. "It's no one! Go wait in the car, honey, it's too hot for you to be outside. I'll be there in a minute."

"Okay, but hurry up," she called back. "We're going to be late if we don't get back on the road, and I'm already double-parked as it is."

My daddy's silky smooth voice broke like a teenager's. "I'll be less than a minute!"

He turned back to me, his face now bright red. "That's Caroline. My wife. We're having a baby boy. Due in September."

I didn't say anything to that. I couldn't. His words were still ringing too loudly in my ears.

No one. He told his pretty blond wife that I was no one.

"Do you want me to walk you back to the contestants' tent before I go? Or . . ." He shrugged his shoulders helplessly.

"I walked over here from a few blocks away. I can do a lot by myself, because I'm mature for my age." My voice broke. "I get straight A's in school, did you know that? I'm smart. And I collect sounds. I'm a good listener. Just like you."

A horn started beeping. It was coming from a red pickup truck a little way down the road. He glanced over at it and then turned back to me.

"I'm so sorry, Maybelle, but I really have to go. Congratulations for singing so nicely . . . and I'm sorry about . . . God. Well, you know. Please wish your mother my best."

Then he tipped his cowboy hat at me, turned his back, and started to walk away.

I stood there, frozen, my mind racing. I had come all this way. I couldn't just let him walk away.

Do something! my brain screamed. *Say something!*

There was only one last thing I could think to try. Magic. Like the kind Momma used that night in New Orleans. I didn't know if I could do it, but I had to try.

So I squeezed my eyes shut. I forced myself to think of all my deepest hopes of getting to know him. My yearnings, my dreams of being a family. Of wanting him to be in my life. Of phone calls, seeing movies together, eating hamburgers and dipping our fries in milkshakes on the hood of his car while the crickets sang to us. I let myself want it all so bad, it felt like the wanting was a real physical thing inside me. I shoved all of those feelings into a tiny ball and cried out.

"Please!"

And I could hardly believe it, but just like that night in New Orleans, the world around us quieted down. Little babies stopped shrieking, dogs stopped barking, bees stopped buzzing. And my daddy stopped walking.

It was working.

He turned around. He looked at me. For the first time, it was like he really *saw* me.

"Please," I said again, my voice barely louder than a whisper.

That tiny, magical word hung between us, as unsure and quivering as a puff of smoke.

He opened his mouth to say something.

But then he closed it. He shook his head and held his

palms toward the sky. "I'm sorry, Maybelle. I'm so sorry. But I can't be the man you want me to be."

I stood there as he got into his shiny red pickup truck with his beautiful wife and their unborn baby boy, and I watched as he drove away.

CHAPTER 29

I stood like that, staring at the empty space where his truck had been, for quite some time. The crowd streamed out of the park all around me. I could almost swear I heard the sound of my heart beating and breaking all at once.

No—one, beat my heart. *You're—no—one.*

Then, when I thought I couldn't sink any lower in this world, I heard the sweetest sound I have ever heard ring out in the air.

"Maybelle! There you are!"

"Momma!" I cried.

She was pushing through the crowd, not even stopping to apologize as she thumped into people and stepped on their shoes.

I ran and vaulted over the metal fence separating the audience area from the stage and started squeezing through the crowd toward her.

She had her guitar slung across her back, and her hair was down, swinging around her tanned shoulders. When we reached each other, I collapsed into her arms. The tears and the words felt like they were coming all at once.

I told her about why I had really come. I told her about my daddy.

"I know," she said quietly. "I saw him."

"Oh, Momma, I've been so stupid. I should have told you the truth about all of this."

She pulled away from me. There were tears in her eyes, and when she spoke, her voice was fierce. "No, I should have told *you* the truth. All these years, I only ever wanted to protect you, but clearly I did it in the worst kind of way. I'm the one who should be sorry."

"Why? Why doesn't he want to know me? It hurts, Momma. It hurts so bad."

Momma started crying, too. We clung on to each other. The crowd bustled around us like a swiftly moving sea.

"Everything will be okay," she said. "I promise."

I'd learned the hard way she wasn't always right—but I hoped she was right about this. I hugged her tighter. "How'd you even get here? I thought you were supposed to be in Miami."

"I was in Miami, but I left in the middle of the night

to get here in time. I was sad about missing it when you first told me about the contest, so when I realized I could make it if I drove all night, I did."

"You drove all that way? For me?"

"I'd fly to the moon for you, Maybelle."

"May! Gemma!"

I looked up. Mrs. Boggs and Tommy were working their way through the crowd, coming straight for us. "What a performance! Even with the incident, you were—" Her smile faded when she caught a look at my tear-stained face. "What's the matter? What happened?"

I couldn't bring myself to look at her. I couldn't say anything. Thankfully, Momma saw I was having trouble, so in a low voice, she explained who the judge was and what had happened.

"I'm so sorry, Mrs. Boggs," I managed to add once Momma was done explaining. Mrs. Boggs's mouth was in a tight, straight line. She was angry, and she had every right to be. "I am so sorry I lied to you. It was a terrible thing to do."

"You have nothing to be sorry about, Maybelle Lane. That man does not deserve you."

I felt someone squeeze my hand. It was Tommy. "Are you okay?" he whispered.

If I talked, I would cry again. So I shrugged.

He squeezed once more, then let go. "Hey, May—where's Pickle?"

Pickle! I'd completely forgotten about him. "He's backstage."

Mrs. Boggs put her arm around me. "Come on. Let's go get that troublemaking dog and get you cleaned up."

After that, I let myself be steered around. We went backstage to collect Pickle—who was quite the surprise to Momma—and signed all the forms that needed signing. Miss Lord seemed close to tears herself once she realized I'd failed. That I'd failed to do what I came here to do.

The RV had not one but two parking tickets when we got back because Mrs. Boggs had parked in such a hurry. I took the longest shower of my life, scrubbing at the hot sauce until my skin was pink and tender. Once I was done, I could tell everyone was trying to be as chipper as possible.

Especially Momma. "Should we go out and eat some barbecue? Or we could skip dinner and go straight to ice cream sundaes," she said, her smile widening by the second.

"Let's do that," Tommy chimed in.

"Or we could go listen to some live music?" Mrs. Boggs said. "Or walk the strip?"

"You know, I'm pretty tired," I told them. "I'd rather just lie down."

"You sure?" Momma asked.

I nodded.

"Why don't you go on into my bedroom," Mrs. Boggs said. "And take Pickle with you. He's freshly bathed and smells good."

"For once," Tommy joked. But I didn't laugh. I couldn't.

And so I stayed in bed, cozied up next to Pickle for the rest of the night. At some point, Momma snuck in to sleep beside me, and that's when I must have drifted off to sleep. When I woke up in the morning, Momma was gone, but I didn't feel like getting out of bed. I let Pickle out so someone could feed him and walk him, but other than that, I didn't feel like eating or doing much of anything at all.

So I didn't.

Around two p.m., there was a knock at the bedroom door. "Hey, May? It's Tommy. Can I come in?"

I shrugged before I realized he couldn't see me. "Sure," I called back, my voice flat. "I guess."

He slipped into the room and shut the door behind him. "How are you?"

I shrugged again.

He pointed at the end of the bed. "Can I sit down?"

"I don't really want to talk about what happened right now, Tommy."

"Well, it's not about you. It's about me. But I'll leave you alone, if that's what you want."

"Wait!" I called out as Tommy turned to leave. "Don't go. If it's about you, then I want to hear every word."

Tommy looked more nervous than I'd ever seen him. He came to sit down, but he barely put any of his weight on the end of the bed. He picked at a loose thread on Mrs. Boggs's quilt.

"So?" I prompted. "What's going on?"

"I wanted to tell you . . . no, I needed to tell you . . . that what you did was brave. Going up onstage like you did, finishing after you fell down, and then going to talk to your daddy. I've been thinking that if you can do something that brave, then . . . I think . . . I think maybe I can, too. That I'm ready. To tell Mrs. Boggs the truth about what's going on. With me. At home."

He said that last part in a whisper. I sat up on my elbows. "You are?"

Tommy nodded. "Yeah. I think I'm going to do it right now so I don't lose my nerve."

"That's great, Tommy. Really great. Do you want me to come with you?"

"No." He squared his shoulders. "This is something I have to do, just me. But I wanted to tell you first. So . . . wish me luck."

"Good luck," I said. "Come get me if you need someone to be there with you after all."

"I will." He went over to the door but stopped before he opened it. "And, May?"

"Yeah?"

"You were amazing yesterday. Even all covered in hot sauce."

"Thanks, Tommy."

"And anyone who doesn't think so should eat a giant sack of cow butts."

"Cow butts?" I repeated, wrinkling my nose.

"Yeah. Cow butts."

He said it with such force and belief, I couldn't help but laugh a little. And it helped push some of the darkness away.

I kept staring at the space where Tommy had been long after he'd left.

Because, somehow, even with all this hurt and failure, I'd still inspired Tommy to go through with the thing he'd been afraid of doing all that time.

I couldn't help but think of *The Wonderful Wizard of Oz*. Sometimes what you think you're missing is actually what you have in spades. Tommy had brains. More brains than me. And despite being known as one of our school's strictest teachers, Mrs. Boggs had a heart. Probably the biggest one I've ever seen.

And me? I had courage. Not from something a wizard gave me, or from a dog, or from a dress made out of stars. Not even from my velvet-voiced daddy.

It was inside me all along.

For the first time since yesterday afternoon, I felt like standing up. Like getting out of bed.

I slipped into the bathroom. I let myself cry about my daddy once more in the shower. The warm water washed my tears away, and by the time I was patting myself dry, I felt a little better.

Once I was finished in the bathroom, I came out in my jean shorts and a T-shirt, my clean hair swinging in a ponytail. I was starting to feel like myself again.

Momma was on the couch, tickling Pickle's stomach. Tommy was sitting next to her, his eyes puffy and red.

"May," Momma breathed when she saw me. I could almost see the relief lighting up the edges of her words. "You're up."

"Yup." I nodded. "I'm up. Where's Mrs. Boggs?"

"She's on the phone outside," Momma said. She put her arm around Tommy's shoulders. "She's helping to put some things in motion."

I slid next to Momma on the couch and flashed Tommy a thumbs-up. "Good. That's really good."

Then I reached down and rubbed Pickle's stomach. "Isn't he great?"

Momma looked from Tommy to Pickle and grinned. "Which one?"

"Both," I said.

"Tommy!" Mrs. Boggs called from outside. "Can you come out here for a minute?"

Tommy took a deep breath before getting up and going outside.

Pickle was so content that he was snoring in Momma's lap. It was the best sound in the whole world, and I hadn't had a chance to capture it yet. I jumped up and rustled around in my bag for my tape recorder.

I pressed the red button. "Pickle snoring," I said in a quiet, clear voice. "Nashville, Tennessee."

"Did you make a new tape?" Momma asked, once I was finished. "From your road trip?"

"I did. Wanna listen?"

"I do."

I grabbed my headphones and plugged them into the jack at the top of the recorder. Momma and I each took an earbud.

We listened to the whole thing. The splash of Tommy's cannonball and the bubbling of his giggles, Pickle's songlike howling, Mrs. Boggs cussing out other drivers in her nice and polite sort of way, the clank of a silver spoon against a fancy ketchup bottle. The carnival music and Tommy and me yelling with joy as we spun in the teacups. As we listened, all the sounds filled me up with a feeling that was bright and full and bursting.

Because, despite everything that had happened—even

with a raw, gnawing ache still inside me—I realized that I'd still managed to capture the sound of happiness.

Once the tape was done, Momma sat back and looked at me, tears in her eyes and a smile spreading across her face. "You know, Maybelle," she said, "I think this may be your best tape yet."

"You know, Momma," I said, leaning into her, "I think you may be right."

EPILOGUE

After spending one last night in Nashville, eating barbecue and listening to live music, Momma, Pickle, and I got ready to head back to Davenport. Tommy was going to drive with Mrs. Boggs, just the two of them.

"It will give us some time to think, make some important phone calls, and form a plan," Mrs. Boggs explained. Tommy looked nervous at her words, but less so once she put a steadying hand on his shoulder.

Momma was able to drive Pickle and me back home all in one day. It was strange seeing the scenery from the week before flashing back at us in one long stretch. It also felt strange that it was just me and Momma again.

But then again, it *wasn't* just me and Momma—or at least it didn't feel that way. I petted Pickle, who was snoring away in my lap. Not anymore.

True to her word, Mrs. Boggs did work out a plan with Tommy and his daddy. Tommy stayed with Mrs. Boggs in her RV for an extra week after they got back.

A few days after we all got back, I heard a loud knocking on Mrs. Boggs's RV door. It was louder than a usual knock, so I went to look through our window. It was Tommy's daddy. He must have come home early from one of his trucking routes.

As soon as Tommy came outside, his daddy bent down and put both of his hands on Tommy's shoulders. I couldn't hear what they were saying, but by the way they hugged at the end of their conversation, rocking back and forth, I had a feeling deep in my heart that things were going to be okay.

After that, Tommy got assigned a caseworker, who came to see him a bunch of times, and Tommy's aunt even came to stay for a while. I liked her a lot. She brought her own dog, who had a doggy wheelchair just like Pickle's. Once the meetings slowed down and Tommy's stepmom had moved out for a while to start counseling, Tommy went back home. A few days after that, Mrs. Boggs asked Tommy and me to come see her.

She told us that she was going to go on her great adventure after all. She'd already put in her notice at school and at Pelican Park. She was going to head north, toward Canada.

"Better late than never, isn't that what people always say?" she asked us, smiling.

Tommy and I were both sad, but in an excited sort of way. She deserved this more than anyone.

"I wanted you to come over because I need help getting rid of all this old stuff." She motioned toward all the cardboard boxes. "Because I don't need it anymore," she said. "But maybe someone else will."

We spent the weekend helping Mrs. Boggs sort through Mr. Boggs's belongings. She gave Tommy all of his old engineering books. And even though she hadn't been planning on getting rid of it, she gave me a handwritten journal of poetry she'd put together herself.

"Now, there's a collection of brilliant minds who knew how to put magic and power into their words, like you did onstage with that beautiful song. Poetry is like music. If anyone can help teach you, it's them."

"And you," I said, holding the journal to my chest. "And Momma. Thank you."

We dropped the rest of the stuff off at a Goodwill on Sunday morning.

Both Tommy and I had trouble saying goodbye to Mrs. Boggs. After Momma threw her a farewell supper, the three of us hugged for a good long time.

"We're like the Three Musketeers, aren't we?" Mrs. Boggs said.

"Who?" Tommy asked.

Mrs. Boggs looked at me. I shrugged. I didn't know who she was talking about, either.

"No. Both of you?" She shook her head. "I'll send you the book in the mail. I'll be expecting a book report."

"Aww," moaned Tommy.

But before Mrs. Boggs left for good, she handed Momma an envelope. When Momma looked inside, she gasped and tried to push it back at Mrs. Boggs. "I can't take this, Alice. It's an incredible gesture, but I can't."

Mrs. Boggs pushed the envelope back at her. "You *can*. To help you get back on your feet. It's exactly what Darryl would have wanted. And it's what I want, too."

"Oh, thank you. Thank you." Momma held the envelope to her chest. "I'll pay you back. I promise you that."

But Mrs. Boggs waved her off. "No. It's a gift, Gemma. All I ask is that you help someone else when you're in the position to. And that you use it well."

And oh, did we use it well. Thanks to Mrs. Boggs's gift and the fact that Momma's musical career started to gain some legs, it wasn't so long before we could afford to move into a little house about half a mile down the road from Pelican Park.

The day we moved out of our trailer, once we had taken all our furniture and boxes of belongings, I tucked my old broken vintage Gran Prix radio at the far back of the highest kitchen cupboard.

It was the only thing I left behind.

I had my own room in our new house. It was tiny, but it was mine. Momma and I spent an entire weekend painting it purple, an even brighter shade than in my old room in Baton Rouge.

I also started a whole new sound collection entitled "Our New Home in Davenport," and so far, the only sound I had recorded was the cheerful singing of the birds outside my bedroom window. I recorded them every morning for weeks and weeks in a row.

I loved those birds. Momma helped me hang a bird feeder outside my window so they would feel welcome and at home. Pickle loved them, too, but for different reasons: he liked to press his nose against the glass and growl at them. He didn't mean any harm, though. Pickle wouldn't know how to hurt a fly.

Some nights I still had trouble falling asleep. Usually it was the memory of my daddy's boots *clomp*ing away from me on the Nashville sidewalk that tormented me. Other times, it was the recollection of the sharp pang of shame I'd felt when I slipped and fell onstage in front of all those people. For months, those events played on repeat in my brain, like a record I couldn't stop spinning.

Then I would think about those birds. I reminded myself they would be there when I woke up, singing their sweet songs to me as the morning sun slanted in through my window. And you know what? They always were.

Tommy had money left over from his scratch-off lottery winnings, so he was able to buy himself a new bike that had better brakes and higher gears. He came over almost every day after school on that bike, rain or shine. Jeremiah tried to give him hell about it, about hanging out with me, but Tommy didn't care, and neither did I. Jeremiah couldn't make me feel alone anymore, because I wasn't. Tommy and I did our homework together, and somehow, about halfway through sixth grade, troublemaking Tommy O'Brien started getting better grades than me.

Even though we said we'd do it for free, Mrs. Boggs sent Tommy and me each five dollars a week to take care of Darryl's grave for her, plus pictures and postcards of all the places she'd been visiting. Twice a week after school, Tommy and I gathered flowers, trimmed the grass around Mr. Boggs's headstone, and read him passages from the books Mrs. Boggs had sent us. Sometimes Tommy talked about things he was building or making, especially the things he had been inspired to create from the old textbooks that used to belong to Mr. Boggs.

Pickle was doing good, too. Momma and I took him to the vet as soon as we could afford a visit. After a long examination and a couple of X-rays, the vet told us, "He's perfectly healthy, but I'm sorry to say this dog will never use his back legs again."

Which was fine by me, as long as he wasn't in any pain. Because Pickle was perfect exactly as he was.

Tommy helped me construct a wooden ramp to our front door to make it easier on Pickle to get around, and even surprised us with a new wheelchair on Christmas. It was less clunky than his first one, with off-road wheels and everything. I don't think I've ever seen a happier dog than Pickle when he first went zooming around in it.

Soon enough, I started singing in the shower again, loud enough for anyone to hear me. I also got up the courage to audition for our school play when tryouts came up in the spring. I was so nervous when my name was called that my hands shook and my palms sweated, but I didn't let that stop me. Not this time. I didn't end up getting cast as the lead, but I had a real good feeling about the next one.

Sixth grade was a mix of changes, heartbreaks, and joys, but eventually, even all that ended as summer came on again. Momma took another job, but not on a cruise ship this time. She was going to be touring the country with a famous singer who needed a backup guitarist.

This time, she told me, I really did have to stay with Cynthia.

I couldn't help but be cross about it. Cynthia had two fluffy cats who I knew would torment Pickle all the live-long day.

The morning Momma was due to leave, I was moping in my room, saying goodbye to my purple walls and to my sweet-singing birds. "See you later," I said gloomily.

And that's when I heard a horn honking outside on the street.

"May!" Momma called. "Your ride's here!"

I gritted my teeth. Cynthia was early. Momma and I hadn't even had our pancake breakfast yet!

As I went into the kitchen to complain, I noticed the loud rumble of the engine outside. It was much louder than a little car's engine should be.

Momma had a smile in her eyes. "You better go see who it is."

I ran outside. It wasn't Cynthia waiting for me in her little red car. It was Mrs. Boggs!

"Hey, sunshine," Mrs. Boggs called as she switched off the RV's engine and came out to meet me. She was wearing a yellow sundress and sparkly silver sandals. "Are you ready for another road trip?"

"Mrs. Boggs!" I cried, racing toward her. I threw myself into her arms. She had grown her hair longer, and she wore her curls free around her face. She even had bright pink lipstick on. "You look so different!"

After rocking me back and forth in a long hug, she held me at arm's length and looked me up and down. "So do you. Taller. Stronger. I like the changes."

I hugged her again. "So do I."

At that exact moment, I saw a flurry of movement from inside the RV. Tommy jumped down onto the pavement, his ratty duffel bag slung over his shoulder. "Hey, May. Surprise!"

"Tommy! Are you coming, too?"

"I wouldn't miss it! And what did they say in the book you made us read, Mrs. Boggs? Oh, yeah—all for one and one for all!"

As Momma fixed pancakes, music filling the air around us, Mrs. Boggs tossed Tommy and me a bunch of worn road maps. "So, my fellow Musketeers. Where should we go this summer? The mountains? New Mexico? Vermont?"

Momma thought we should go to California and lie out on the beach. Tommy wanted to go to New York City to see Times Square and eat a slice of authentic New York pizza.

I couldn't decide where I wanted to go. Honestly, I didn't really care. We'd have fun as long as we were together. And you know what?

I planned on singing the whole way.

ACKNOWLEDGMENTS

When first setting out, writing a book can feel like a lonely endeavor. So much time spent alone with your thoughts and your pen and your hopes of what the story might turn out to be. But as I gained courage to share Maybelle's story with the world, I found that the process of creating a book is anything *but* lonely: so many talented people had their hands on these words to make it what it is today.

I'd like to begin by thanking my agent, Pete Knapp, who wrote me a letter so lovely after he first read this book that I burst into tears and hugged my laptop to my chest (truly). Pete, your thoughtfulness, professionalism, and all-around wonderfulness continue to amaze me. I have lost count of the times I've said to my husband, "Wow. Pete really is the best." Thank you for guiding my career with such a steady, encouraging hand.

To Abigail Koons, Ema Barnes, Blair Wilson, and the rest of the team at Park & Fine Literary and Media, thank you for all your behind-the-scenes work that made this book possible. Thank you also to Mary Pender-Coplan at UTA for your enthusiasm and continued advocacy of this story.

An enormous thank-you to Mary Kole, whose sharp editorial

eye and superb manuscript notes deepened the characters and made me think critically about every aspect of this story, no matter how small. Working with you has been an utter delight.

Thank you to Nancy Siscoe, my brilliant editor at Knopf, for sending kind notes and tins of cookies exactly when I needed them most. Each remark you make about craft or story is a pearl of wisdom I write down and revisit often. I have learned so much from working with you.

Thank you also to the amazing team at Penguin Random House who made this book possible, especially Marisa DiNovis, Alison Kolani, Artie Bennett, Jake Eldred, Trish Parcell, April Ward, and Natalia Dextre. Thank you to the fantastic people in marketing and publicity, including Adrienne Waintraub, Kristin Schulz, Shaughnessy Miller, Kelly McGauley, Dominique Cimina, and Noreen Herits.

A special thanks to Brittany Williams and TJ Duckworth for your thoughtful read-throughs.

To Leslie Mechanic and Helen Crawford-White, thank you for my gorgeous cover. And thank you for the stars! I love them so much.

Thank you to the many writers I met at workshops and conferences, especially Darcey Rosenblatt, whose enthusiasm for the first page inspired me to dig down and finish the first draft. Thank you to so many of my wonderful friends who were here for me during the process of writing this book, but in particular Amanda Glassman and Katherine Lin, for hours of brainstorming, advice, and retreat company.

To Haddon Cord, songwriter and singer extraordinaire, thank you for lending an eye to the lyrics and breathing real, musical life into Momma's song, which I listened to on repeat during revisions.

To my sister, Lael, thank you for going on the road trip with me, where we drove almost exactly the same route that Maybelle takes. I will never forget laughing with you in the tiny back seat of our rental car as we ate fried chicken in the Walmart parking lot. I am so lucky you're my sister.

Mom and Dad, thank you for always encouraging me to follow my dreams and telling me unabashedly to do what I love. To Patrick, Lauren, Pierce, and Maeve, thank you for all the love and support. Thank you to my grandmother, Gammy, who read this book in one sitting and sent me the loveliest letter about it afterward, and to my mother-in-law, Joy Carrigan, for being such a spirited cheerleader for both me and this book.

Rachel Richardson and David Roderick, you are pillars of the Berkeley literary community. I'm so grateful for your friendship, as well as your stewardship of Left Margin LIT, which is the warm and inclusive creative workspace of my dreams. Thanks for always having a hot pot of coffee brewing.

I'm thankful for my dog, Mo, for her stalwart companionship, sleeping in the armchair behind me as I write (and for reminding me that taking breaks and going for long walks in the woods are good for me, too).

And finally, to my husband, Chris: thank you for reading early drafts, for picking me up off the floor when I felt I couldn't move forward and telling me to trust the process, for feeding me chocolate and pizza and wine whenever I needed it most, for celebrating every little victory along the way, for having faith in me that has been unshakable, from the very beginning. You have always been my biggest champion, and I couldn't be more grateful. I love you, Dub.

At the moment of writing this, I have yet to lay my hands on a finished copy of this book—but when I do, I will thumb through the pages quickly and listen to them whirring and I will know that this, to me, is the sound of happiness.

Thank you for reading!